ACROSS THE CHINA SEA

Also available in English by Gaute Heivoll

Before I Burn

ACROSS THE CHINA SEA

A Novel

Gaute Heivoll

Translated from the Norwegian by Nadia Christensen

Graywolf Press

This publication is made possible, in part, by the voters of Minnesota through a Minnesota State Arts Board Operating Support grant, thanks to a legislative appropriation from the arts and cultural heritage fund, and a grant from the Wells Fargo Foundation. Significant support has also been provided by Target, the McKnight Foundation, the Lannan Foundation, the Amazon Literary Partnership, and other generous contributions from foundations, corporations, and individuals. To these organizations and individuals we offer our heartfelt thanks.

This translation has been published with the financial support of NORLA.

Published by Graywolf Press
250 Third Avenue North, Suite 600
Minneapolis, Minnesota 55401

All rights reserved.

www.graywolfpress.org

Published in the United States of America

ISBN 978-1-55597-784-9

2 4 6 8 9 7 5 3 1
First Graywolf Printing, 2017

Library of Congress Control Number: 2017930110

Cover design: Jeenee Lee Design

Cover photo: Augustus E. Martin. Courtesy of the Lenox Library Association. This work is licensed for use under a Creative Commons Attribution License (CC BY).

To Anita

ACROSS THE CHINA SEA

PART ONE

1.

In the fall of 1994, while clearing out the house and emptying the writing desk in the living room, I discovered the contract Papa had signed that evening in February 1945. I also found a number of other papers related to caregiving, among them my own letters. There were three photographs of Mama too: one of her standing in front of the Parliament building, another in front of the Royal Palace, and a third beside the bronze lion outside the Kunstnernes Hus art gallery. Except for the pictures, which were tucked inside Mama's confirmation Bible, everything was in a brown envelope that had been taped shut. On the envelope were the words *Caregiving Papers*. It was Papa's handwriting.

The contract had been drawn up by the Stavanger Child Welfare office and signed in duplicate. It stated that Mama and Papa agreed to provide care for five mentally disabled children, for which they would receive eighty *kroner* a month per child. Perhaps they got the same amount for Josef, Matiassen, and Christian Jensen. I don't know. Perhaps it was more. After all, they weren't children.

The document went on to say that Child Welfare would pay for clothing and footwear, as well as for potential doctor visits and medicine.

Furthermore, Papa and Mama promised to:

Provide the children with sufficient, healthy food
Give the children a good, secure place to sleep in their own beds
Keep the children clean and neat
Adapt the children's work to their ages and abilities

That was all. Four points.

The children's names and birthdates followed. Lilly. Nils. Erling. Ingrid. Sverre. Sverre was only four years old. There were thirteen years between Sverre and Lilly. She was almost grown up. All had been baptized in St. Johannes parish in Stavanger.

Required termination notice: one month.

The contract was yellowed and full of spots; snowflakes had probably melted on the paper while Papa signed it by the light of Matiassen's old miner's lantern. Papa's shaky signature. The Stavanger Child Welfare stamp. And the date, February 17, 1945.

I remember that it was snowing.

There was a cover letter too. It described the living conditions of the five children before they came to us, and was based largely on a Child Welfare report. The letter was typed on one A4 sheet of paper and attached to the contract with a paper clip. Rust from the paper clip had rubbed off onto the page. The typewritten words were faint and unclear, so I stood by the window to read them.

It was like taking a deep breath.

And then.

The five children had been taken from an apartment in Stavanger near the *gata*, or street, known as Strandgata on December 22, 1944, after several people had independently expressed concern for the strange, large family. They said you could smell the stench from the apartment the moment you entered the building. So just before Christmas, the Stavanger Child Welfare office sent an inspector to investigate. When he knocked, one of the children opened the door; I imagine it was Ingrid, because the report stated that several of them had *inadequately developed language skills*. It must have been Ingrid. After all, she had never been able to speak a word. Perhaps she stood in the doorway licking her lips, perhaps she howled softly.

Perhaps she made a deep, dignified curtsy the way Lilly had taught her, and stepped aside.

The report was written in ink by a man named Aarrestad. He had knocked on the door and taken off his hat when he entered. Afterward he went home and wrote that during his thirteen years with Stavanger Child Welfare he had never seen anything worse. He was the first to liken them to animals.

Inside the apartment the foul odor was almost unbearable, he wrote. Garbage and trash of every sort, filth, mouse-eaten mattresses, mildewed curtains and newspaper covering the windows. Stinking utter chaos. The man of the house, stonemason Hertinius Olsen, slumped apathetically in a chair while the children crawled around his feet. The children's mother, Rebekka, stood in a corner of the room, apparently trying to put together a meal, or perhaps she was trying to hide the fact that there was no food in the apartment.

Perhaps she was ashamed.

The report further stated that Hertinius and Rebekka Olsen— who, like their five children, were described as mentally disabled— had not managed to use their ration cards properly. They were no longer capable of providing food, either for themselves or for their flock of children. By the time Aarrestad knocked on the door, they had given up. Aarrestad ended his report with these words: *The seven live like animals, under the most ignoble conditions. The children are like animals, with animal habits, and therefore it is recommended that Child Welfare intervene immediately in the case of this poor family.*

The children were taken away the following evening.

The weather in Stavanger was calm, cold, and clear. Darkness had fallen, the streets were decorated for Christmas. A few stars shone above the fjord, and there was a thin layer of ice on Lake Breiavannet. The five siblings were driven through the city to the Child Welfare office located at 26 Nygata, not far from St. Petri church. There they were lined up in a row and led through the corridors. They got washed and scrubbed and, at the end, deloused. They were given new clothes, which only partially fit them, but were better than the rags they had before. The two girls got their hair braided, the three boys got a haircut.

No one protested.

On Christmas Eve 1944 they sat for the first time at a table that had been set properly and were served a steaming-hot Christmas meal at Child Welfare expense. Meanwhile, Rebekka and Hertinius Olsen sat alone in the miserable apartment near Strandgata without their five children. Suddenly there was silence all around them. No one pestered them for something to eat. No one crawled across the floor making animal-like sounds. Hertinius and Rebekka would never get their children back. I don't know how they reacted. Perhaps they protested.

The report does not say.

There proved to be no care facility in Rogaland County with the capacity to take in five mentally disabled siblings. It took until late January 1945 before a solution was found. The welfare office contacted care facilities up the coast all the way north to Bergen, along the fjords, and inland across Ryfylke County. But that was before they were told about my parents, both trained as nurses, and about our house in a small parish in southern Norway, forty kilometers from the coast.

After that, everything moved quickly.

The formalities were completed, a contract with four points covering all five children was worked out, and as with the cover letter, everything fit on one page.

I don't know what the five imagined when they were picked up one morning several weeks later. Maybe they had been told where they were going. Maybe not. Maybe someone told Lilly. She was seventeen years old and perhaps not even mentally disabled, just low IQ; from now on, she would be like a mother for the four other children. Maybe someone told her, maybe she nodded and acted as if she understood.

They had no luggage, no possessions, just the new clothes they were wearing. Lilly gathered the siblings around her, the Child Welfare workers said good-bye, and then the five were led out to the street and into the black car waiting for them.

Rain and sleet showers drifted across the leaden fjord, but when they came to the Jæren seashore, the weather cleared and they could see how the ocean curved at the horizon.

They drove through Egersund and Flekkefjord, across the Kvinesheia uplands, and at the highest point they could have turned and caught a final glimpse of the sea in the distance.

It was a trip of more than two hundred kilometers.

When they got to Mandal it was already dark. They turned north and continued along the Mandalselva River. The weather grew colder, the snowbanks along the road became higher, and soon they were driving through dark forests; in the searching gleam of the head-lights the snow had a bluish glow.

I remember the shimmering headlights that approached from the bottom of the hill, and the car that drove up and turned into the farmyard as I stood with Tone and Josef in the doorway of our house. I remember the moment the driver opened the back door and the first to appear in the light was Lilly. She was eight years older than me, and I thought she was a grown woman. Her hair hung down her back in a long braid; she ducked her head, and stepped out of the car into the snow. She looked like other women I knew, and in the glow of the old miner's lantern she was almost beautiful. She stood next to Mama, seeming shy and reserved. The two women were the same height. They looked at each other and shook hands, and Lilly curtsied so deeply that her coat spread out on the snow. Then she turned and shouted something into the car, and the siblings got out, one after another; first Nils, then Erling, then Ingrid, and finally little Sverre. At the end they all stood in the snow. It was an odd group, they seemed strange and completely out of place. Nils, who was the second-oldest, but taller than Lilly, wore pants that hung loose at the waist and he pulled them up with his hands in his pockets. He stood beside Mama, grinning, as if someone had just told him an improbable story and he'd almost understood the point. The three youngest children held on to each other: Sverre seemed frightened and clung to Ingrid, who clasped Erling's hand. Ingrid's mouth was half-open, as if she were screaming or laughing. But she was doing neither, she was completely quiet. Erling's head wobbled as he kicked the snow with the tip of his shoe and stole a cautious sidelong glance at Papa. Papa was wearing a winter coat from his years at Dikemark and an old beret. He leaned over the hood of the car and signed the contract on the warm surface. Then he gave a copy of the contract to the driver, and afterward he rubbed his hands together. I saw the snow swirling in the glow of the miner's lantern.

"Is it them?" Tone whispered.

I nodded.

"It's them," I said. "They're here now."

I felt a cold draft on my feet. Papa took a few steps forward, and Mama stood next to him in the well-worn sweater Anna had given her. The bluish-white light from the lantern surrounded them like a heavenly glow. It made me think of the wedding picture hanging above the piano in the living room, in which Papa has his hands behind his back and Mama sits in front of him on a chair with her bouquet in her lap to hide the fact that she is pregnant. They are both smiling in the picture. They now stood with their backs to me as the headlights of the stranger's car lit up the ash tree. I could see a little of the hay barn and the snow-covered fields that gently rose and fell until they disappeared at the edge of the forest. Snow drifted down from the vast, dark heavens. I heard Papa's voice as he leaned toward Mama and said something only she could hear. And none of us had the slightest idea of what was ahead.

2.

When Papa was twenty years old he left home to become a deacon, a profession that combined nursing and social work. Early one morning he took the "Arendal" train on the long trip from Kristiansand to Oslo, where he went to Diakonhjemmet hospital, which was northwest of the city center at Steinerud, an old estate surrounded by fields, meadows, and oak forests. There he learned to care for patients in a *Christlike spirit of love,* as they put it. He left home and became a deacon, and that was highly unusual. Hardly anyone left the parish. And certainly not to go to Oslo. If someone left, it was mostly for America, usually in order to earn money or to stay there forever, unless you came back because you had lost your sanity.

Papa was at Steinerud for six months. Then he got a job at Dikemark psychiatric hospital, where he stayed for eleven years. For eleven years he worked with the insane and mentally disabled, and they were eleven good years. At Dikemark there were young boys who howled like wolves at night; there were people who could not walk, sit upright, hold a spoon, or speak; there were older men who believed they were emperors or military commanders, murderers or Christ on the cross. And then there was Eugen Olsen, who was sure that every building where he lived was on fire. Papa loved them all. Working with the insane and mentally disabled was what gave meaning to his life. He had left his rural parish and, for the time being, did not think of going back. The eleven years at

Dikemark became the eleven happiest years of his life. I can hear him say it himself: *That was when I felt alive.*

That was when he felt alive, and it was there, at Dikemark, he met Mama. After several years as a nurse at Ullevål hospital she had successfully applied for a position at Dikemark in the women's unit, which was separate from the men's unit but inside the same high fence. The units were reminiscent of venerable manor houses and had names like the Guest House, the Treatment House, the View, and the Castle. From a distance it looked like an old aristocratic estate, with walking paths and a small park. Almost normal, aside from the fence.

Living quarters for the staff were located some distance from the stately treatment units, and it was while walking to and from the night shift that Mama and Papa became acquainted. While they walked beside each other in the dark, she told him about her father, who was the custodian at the Foreign Ministry housing complex on Parkveien, just behind the Royal Palace in Oslo. It was winter, moonlight sparkled on the icy snowbanks along the road, and she told him one of her earliest memories: Uncle Josef standing in the middle of the room in the custodian apartment, singing. They walked together to the staff apartments and lingered awhile in the darkness before unlocking their respective doors. After the next night shift they walked together again. It went on this way until one night Mama stopped at the darkest part of the road. No streetlight. No moon. No stars. Mama stood still, but Papa continued walking for a while before he discovered he was alone. He stopped, turned around, and saw her like a dark shadow, a motionless form darker than the darkness itself.

"Karin?" he said.

She did not reply.

He walked toward her, but she did not say anything; she just waited until he was very close, and then she put her arms around him.

One of Mama's earliest memories was of Uncle Josef singing. Later, Josef would be sent to a care facility in Røyken parish, and Mama began to take singing lessons from a woman in the Frogner neighborhood in Oslo. She planned to become a singer—she was encouraged to practice, and told she could go as far as she wished. But when her mother died, Mama stopped abruptly. Instead, she became a nurse. I don't know what happened. It was as if she suddenly realized that singing had been the wrong track. Better to care for the sick than to sing, to work with the mentally and physically disabled rather than with impresarios. It was as if she suddenly understood.

Perhaps it was Josef who got her to start singing. Perhaps it was because of him that she bought a large, black Steinway concert piano with her inheritance from Grandma, and perhaps it was memories of Uncle Josef that made her think of applying to Dikemark.

Uncle Josef was mentally disabled, after all.

My great-grandfather had been a coach driver at the Granfoss Brug paper mill in Lysaker. People said Josef fell out of the carriage and hit his head, and hadn't been himself since. He had been talented, no question about that; then he fell, his head struck a rock, and he became a different person. In school he was quickly labeled mentally disabled, but one thing did not change: his deep, resounding singing voice. While still living with his father in Oslo, he sang in the Hope Chorus, which had gone on a concert tour to the city of Trondheim. Exactly where they performed, no one knew for certain. Uncle Josef could not say much about the trip, aside from two memorable events: in Trondheim he met a woman whom he called *my young bride*, and he saw the midnight sun above Nidaros Cathedral at two o'clock in the afternoon.

Josef was there in the doorway with Tone and me that evening in February 1945 when the siblings from Stavanger stood by the car in the snow. He had come downstairs from his room, which was above the entrance to the house and overlooked the ash tree. He had put on his uniform jacket, but had forgotten the medal for courage. Now he stood barefoot on a rag rug and saw the same thing we did.

"So these are the new crazies," he said.

The siblings looked as if they had traveled twice across the Atlantic like Jensen and Matiassen, who by now had gone to bed upstairs. Lilly lined up the children—from Nils, who was the tallest, to Sverre, who was the smallest—and Papa shook hands with each one. They bowed politely, except for Erling, who just wobbled his head, and Ingrid, who curtsied almost as deeply and elegantly as Lilly. The whole time, the driver had stood shivering; now he got into the car and started the engine. The headlights came on, and again I could see the fields and the edge of the forest where the pine trees seemed to stiffen in the sudden light.

Papa glanced toward the house and saw Josef, Tone, and me standing in the doorway. A thought seemed to cross his mind. He gave us a little smile, and for a moment appeared almost ashamed, as if we had seen something we must never reveal to anyone else. The driver turned the car in a wide arc, the headlights cut through the darkness, straight into my eyes, and the night smelled of snow and exhaust fumes as we heard the car disappear down the hill. For a moment we were all left to ourselves. Papa carefully folded the contract, Mama swung Matiassen's lantern.

"We'll go inside now," she said.

Mama went first, holding the lantern in her hand, Papa was last with the contract sticking out of his coat pocket, and between them, the whole flock of siblings came walking toward our house.

3.

Papa had always intended to move back to his childhood parish—despite the happy years at Dikemark—and after almost twelve years on the east coast he thought it was finally time. He'd had his eleven happy years, he had married a girl from the heart of Oslo who was also a nurse, and several months after the wedding their first child was born.

I was born in the autumn at the maternity clinic in Asker, and at first I slept in an old orange crate that once had been shipped across the China Sea. Papa had found the crate in the attic above the men's unit, along with old sedan chairs, straitjacket beds, and other paraphernalia from the past. I don't know why he took the orange crate, but he was allowed to keep it, and Mama made it into a baby bed. The same autumn we moved into a larger apartment in Drengsrud, not far from the Dikemark asylum, and I lived there for the first years of my life. I remember a few incidents from that time, but beginning with the war I remember almost everything.

On April 9, 1940, the day the Germans invaded, there was still snow on the ground after a long winter. My shoes were dirty; I stood in the yard outside the staff apartments and threw snowballs at the German planes that swooped in low over the mountain ridges. I remember the Steinway piano, but I don't remember Mama or Papa or anyone else playing it. The piano stood against a wall with the cover closed over the keys, and Mama said it was much too heavy to be moved. But it got carried down the stairs anyway, and stood in the yard covered with a tarpaulin when all our things were packed and we were ready to leave.

Mama and Papa had made plans for our new life in the south of Norway. They would build a big house with many rooms and large windows. Sunlight would stream in from morning till evening; the steps leading upstairs would be wide and low, so people didn't have to lift their legs very high. The kitchen would be spacious, with enough room to prepare food for many people. The house would be built to accommodate caring for patients—the mentally ill or disabled who needed assistance—and that way they could continue the Dikemark work in a *Christlike spirit of love*. They would build their own little asylum in the midst of the parish where Papa was born and grew up, a place Mama had not yet seen.

Just before the war, Papa took the train south several times. When he returned home he brought long rolls of paper that covered the entire kitchen table when he spread them out; he explained everything, and Mama lifted me up so I could see too. The house would be in the middle of the parish, just one kilometer from the store and the Christian meetinghouse. An old, drafty house had once stood on the property; it had been Papa's childhood home, but had burned to the ground in the spring before the war. During the summer and fall the new house was built on the ruins of the old one. The rooms were large and light, just as planned, with space for beds along the walls; the windows faced east and south and west; the steps leading upstairs were wide and low, just like the drawings; the doors had large handles, and could be locked only from the outside. And when everything was finished, the war broke out.

The house was what they had imagined, what they had dreamed of: their own little Dikemark, with the same pine trees outside, but without a fence, and without bars on the windows. Our new house lay at the edge of the forest, with gently rolling fields around it and a road that wound right through the farmyard and on to the neighboring farm where a childless couple, Hans and Anna, lived. Hans worked the farm and Anna was musically gifted, almost like Mama; she played the old reed organ in the church balcony for Sunday services, Papa told us. At the bottom of the road was the milk platform, where dairy trucks picked up full milk cans and dropped off empty ones, and from there the country road continued toward the store and the meetinghouse and the doctor's office, which also served as the public library. In the spring the road was muddy and rutted with deep wheel tracks, while in the summer, dust from the road drifted sideways with the wind. Several hundred meters north of the house was a lake where you could go swimming.

I already saw it in my mind.

This is what the new world was like.

Our own asylum, in the midst of the forest, in the midst of the parish, forty kilometers from the coast. But without patients at the moment; at the moment there was just the Steinway piano, the Junghans clock Mama and Papa got as a wedding present, the old orange crate from the attic at Dikemark, and me. And there was Tone, who still lay in Mama's stomach.

4.

I know the sun was shining the day we left, because I remember the way our shadows stretched across the yard and seemed to consider how far they dared to go with us. It was the middle of May, I'd seen long columns of German soldiers in town, and the trees were just beginning to turn green as we sat on the train headed toward Drammen. Through the window I saw the harbor, the huge cranes standing motionless in the shimmering heat, and the sea sparkling around the cargo boats along the pier. Some snow still remained on the hills west of the river. The train stopped with a jolt; people got on board, shoved suitcases onto the luggage racks, took off their coats and hung them on hooks by the windows. We continued farther inland, but when we got to Kongsberg the bridge across the Lågen River had been blown up, so everyone had to get out and go on foot. Papa put me down onto the crushed rock and we had to walk a long way along the tracks and then on the road, until finally we crossed the river below the demolished bridge. The water was flowing rapidly, sunlight glittered like silver on its muddy surface; Mama held Papa's arm tightly, and everyone could see she was pregnant. We waited on the other side of the river for a new train that would take us farther south. Mama sat down on the suitcase, Papa whistled softly to himself, and I thought about the new life waiting for us somewhere at the end of the train tracks.

We rode through sparse pine forests and past marshlands still brown after the winter. White wooden houses, farmyards with moldering mounds of snow, and small, newly plowed fields streamed past the window. I ran back and forth in the train, but each time it hurtled through a tunnel I curled up by Mama's feet and sat there until we were out in the light.

Late in the evening we reached Kristiansand. I could smell the sea, and I saw that the ships along the pier were dark because of the wartime blackout. We stayed overnight at Hotel Bondeheimen, next to Børs Park. There were just two beds in the room, and I slept with Mama that night. It took me a long time to get to sleep; the mattress smelled strange, I heard the sounds of the city. Mama lay close behind me, I felt her large, warm stomach against my back and her even breathing on my neck.

The next day we continued by bus from the central square, where the cathedral spire had been shattered during the bombing in April, and west of the city we saw the harbor entrance and the vast ocean beyond. We had seen German soldiers in Kristiansand, but there were fewer as we got farther from the city. The bus drove west at first, then turned north and headed inland. I don't know what I'd imagined, but when we neared Papa's home parish I had the strange feeling that I'd been there before. The hills were the same as back in Drengsrud, the sun glistened on the same lakes, and the forest was the same as the thick, dark woods behind the Castle at Dikemark. It was almost like coming home. Long, tranquil mountain ridges rose green and dark blue in the distance, and when we came down the hill by Lake Livannet I saw the parish for the first time. We rode slowly past the Brandsvoll meetinghouse, which at the time was filled with elderly people who needed care after being evacuated from a nursing home in town. When we got to the fork in the road, the bus stopped in front of the store and I looked in the windows at the counter and the shelves and the sacks of seed grain—but what I noticed most was the elegant balcony that hung out over the road.

Several hundred meters farther west, we drove over the Djupåna River and continued across the rolling hills past the home of the church sexton, Reinert Sløgedal. I looked at Mama, I looked at Papa, who had stopped whistling long ago. He just sat watching the road. I realized we had arrived when I saw the milk platform he had talked about. The bus slowed down, it stopped, the door swung open, I smelled road dust and horse manure, and when we got out, Anna and Hans were there to meet us.

Mama came down the steps heavily with Papa holding her arm, and he didn't let go until she stood among the yellow dandelions at the side of the road. Then, while the engine idled, he got our two suitcases, and when the bus finally drove away, there wasn't a sound.

"Is this the end of the world?" Mama asked.

Hans and Anna had been standing on the other side of the road, and now calmly came toward us. Papa glanced at Mama. Hans ran his hand through his hair. Then Anna began to laugh.

"Yes. Welcome to the end of the world," she said.

Anna laughed, Mama laughed, Hans ran his fingers through his hair again and spat to the side, and then they all shook hands. Hans had brought his horse harnessed to a cart; the front wheels were at a slant and cast delicate shadows in the grass. Papa slung the suitcases onto the cart, and the four of us climbed into the back. I smelled the horse, my feet dangled in the air, and I remember Mama's sudden laughter when the horse jerked in the shafts, how she grabbed Papa's arm and held tight as the creaking wheels began to roll.

I remember the laughter, the wind in the trees, the cart wheels' flickering shadows, and I remember that when we reached the house Mama stood in the garden under the ash tree. Everything was about the way I had imagined it, except for the hayloft, which stood there from before, the outhouse—a small, chilly cubicle with two black holes above the empty manure cellar—and the ash tree, which was old and moss covered and surely had been there for hundreds of years.

Papa hadn't said a word about the ash tree.

We walked around the house from room to room while Mama murmured softly to herself. Papa went first, then Mama, and I followed right behind. We went slowly up the stairs to the second floor, into the rooms on the right, into the rooms on the left, then down the stairs again, into the space that would be the kitchen, into the front hall, into what would be the living room. The whole time, Mama walked ahead of me talking softly to herself. I don't know whether it was from disappointment or enthusiasm, but finally she sat down on a backless stool that had been left in the middle of the floor and that still showed the carpenters' shoeprints. She just sat there with her hands in her lap, staring straight ahead.

Maybe she had imagined something else. Maybe she was disappointed. Maybe she was just tired. She was six months pregnant.

That stool would later become Matiassen's stool. Our own furniture arrived a few days later by horse and cart from town. The orange crate, the wall clock, the Steinway piano. Hans delivered everything with his horse. The cart stood in the middle of the yard with wood blocks under the wheels while Papa and Hans, with the help of several men from neighboring farms, maneuvered the heavy piano up the front steps and into the living room.

Before long, we had two cows in the barn stalls, Papa bought a horse with long, bristly hair that hung down over its eyes, and Anna gave Mama a thick sweater to wear in the barn. After just a few weeks Matiassen and Jensen came from the Eg asylum in Kristiansand, and later Uncle Josef moved from the Røyken care facility. He was then about fifty years old, skinny as a rail, but he had a broad smile in the picture on his Border Resident card, and he was overjoyed to see Mama again.

"My dear little Karin," he shouted when he arrived in the yard. "Is this really where you live?"

"Yes," Mama replied. "Who would have believed it?"

Josef set down his small suitcase and went over to her.

"Can I get a hug?"

He always had his Border Resident card in his jacket pocket, even long after the war was over; it would gradually become tattered and worn at the edges, but in the picture his smile was as broad as ever. By August that first year of the war Josef had settled into the room above the front entrance, while Jensen and Matiassen shared the room that faced east toward the forest, and at long last we could begin our new life.

5.

More than four years later, on that evening in February 1945, we accompanied the siblings from Stavanger upstairs to the large room prepared for them. Papa had painted the walls pale green, Mama had scrubbed the floor, five beds were set up along the walls, and in the middle of the room stood a kitchen table and chairs. It had become a kind of home. Mama had put a cloth on the table along with five new tin plates; Papa had hammered a nail in the wall between the windows and hung a picture of Our Lord with a shepherd's staff and a lamb in his arms.

"This is where we thought you'd live," said Papa. He turned on the light and ushered them in.

The five followed him. Sverre clung to Lilly's skirt, Nils kept his hands in his pockets to hold up his pants, and Erling stood as he had in the yard, his head wobbling rhythmically as if from a foolish thought he could not escape.

"Here are the beds," Papa went on. "And you can eat here at the table."

"Will we get food?" Lilly asked.

"Yes, of course you'll get food," Papa replied.

The five stared at Papa as he went over to the table and pulled out a chair. Tone and I stood just behind Josef and peered through the doorway. It was as if nothing the siblings saw made any impression on them. They just looked wide-eyed at Papa, who was now sitting on the chair. I glanced at Ingrid, who seemed about the same age as me, or perhaps a little younger. Her eyes were slanted, her hair bristly, her cheeks ruddy, and she licked herself around the mouth.

"I hope you'll like it here," said Papa, getting to his feet.

Nils went straight over to the chair, sat down with satisfaction, took his hands out of his pockets, and crossed his arms. Erling walked over to one of the beds and sat down on it. Papa looked at Lilly, then at Mama, and at Lilly again. She stepped forward.

"Can we eat now?" she asked.

Fifty years later the tin plates showed up again. I found them neatly stacked in the storage room under the stairs when I cleared out the house. There were ten of them. Matiassen's lantern was there in the darkness too, with a cracked glass. The plates were dented and thick with dust, and as I held one in my hands I saw in my mind the five sitting at the table. For us downstairs, the siblings' meals were always accompanied by a terrible racket: scraping chair legs, clattering cutlery, minor squabbles, and general pandemonium. It felt as if the table and chairs and soup plates and everything else might crash through the floor at any moment. But at some point they always grew quiet. At some point they all found their places around the table, Lilly dished up the soup, and then they sang a table grace. Everyone sang, except for Ingrid, who howled softly, and they always sang "Blessed Lord, Be Our Guest." After the table grace, the scraping and clattering and bickering continued until the meal was finished, and then Lilly put the tin plates and cups and utensils on a tray and carried everything down to the kitchen.

That's what always happened, beginning with their very first meal upstairs that evening. Mama and Papa brought the food up to them, and when they were finished Lilly gathered up the tin plates and came downstairs to the kitchen.

"Thank you for the food, ma'am," she said, and curtsied deeply with the tray still in her hands.

"You're welcome," said Mama as she took the tray.

Then Lilly disappeared upstairs, and I wondered who in the world had taught them to sing so well.

They had come to a new world. The snow lay a meter deep outside the house and woodlands stretched in every direction as far as the eye could see. The ocean, which they were used to in Stavanger, was far away; the closest thing to it was Lake Djupesland, which still lay white and silent several hundred meters north of the house. Mama and Papa were busy with the siblings that entire evening, and after Tone and I had gone to bed in our small room we lay very still and listened to all the new sounds filling the house. Running children's feet, bedlam and bawling, furniture shoved back and forth across the floor. The floorboards overhead seemed to sway in time with the hullabaloo. But then things calmed down, and finally there was complete silence. The door closed softly, Mama and Papa came downstairs, and it was clear that the siblings had gone to bed.

"What are they doing now?" Tone whispered beside me.

"I think they're saying their prayers," I replied.

It was quiet for a long time. We lay there without moving and listened, almost like when we occasionally heard English bombers roaring in from the sea in the southwest. But this time no airplane approached. It was absolutely quiet upstairs, but we listened anyway. And then we heard Lilly singing. Lilly sang, Erling and Sverre sang, and Nils sang in falsetto, so he sounded like a child too. It was some sort of prayer, an evening song, but I couldn't make out the words. When the song ended, we heard quiet footsteps. It was Lilly: she went over to the door and switched off the light, then walked across the floor in the dark and lay down in her bed.

6.

The next day Tone and I were upstairs with the siblings. It must have been a Sunday because Papa was at church with Josef and Jensen, Matiassen was alone in his room rocking on his stool, and Mama was busy downstairs in the kitchen. Tone and I stole up the stairs and I knocked on the door. After a moment's silence, we heard footsteps approaching. We glanced at each other. At that moment I was sorry we stood there, but it was too late. The door opened slowly. A face appeared. It was Lilly.

"Can we come in?" asked Tone.

Lilly gave her a distrustful look.

"Why?" she said.

"We were wondering about something," said Tone.

"About what?"

"Just something," said Tone.

Lilly regarded us for a long time; I thought she was going to shut the door in our faces, but then she stepped aside and let us in. Sverre sat on the floor playing with the fringe on the rug, Nils lay on one of the beds staring at the ceiling as he ran his hand slowly through his hair, Erling sat on his chair by the table, and Ingrid stood gazing out the window.

It was like going into a stranger's house.

"We wondered if Ingrid and Erling wanted to come outside with us," said Tone.

Ingrid turned around, Erling looked up. Nils sat up in bed. They looked at us in surprise, then at Lilly.

"Ingrid and Erling?" said Lilly

"Yes," Tone replied cheerfully. "Can they come?"

Perhaps eight seconds went by. Then Lilly nodded.

"Okay," she said. "But no crying."

We took them down the stairs and out into the yard. As we led them through the snow, Tone held Ingrid's hand, I held Erling's, and for a long time all four of us stood under the ash tree, about where Matiassen put his stool during the summer. It had snowed all night. But now the clouds had disappeared, the weather had cleared, and Tone, Ingrid, Erling, and I made the very first tracks in the smooth, white expanse. Our cheeks froze and the snow crunched under our feet. Blue smoke swirled from the chimney at Hans and Anna's house, but there was no sign of anyone. Tone pulled her hands into the arms of her coat. We heard the frozen branches of the ash tree creaking above us.

"Should we play a game?" Tone asked.

Neither Ingrid nor Erling answered. The snow was ankle deep, a frigid wind blew right through our clothes, and Ingrid and Erling just stood there.

"What should we play?" Tone said.

No one replied. Tone looked at me, and I shrugged my shoulders. Then Tone pointed to the house.

"Uncle Josef lives up there," she said. "And Jensen and Matiassen live in the room next to him. Matiassen is crazy, and so is Jensen. But they aren't dangerous, so you don't have to be afraid."

Ingrid and Erling still stood silently in the snow, but both seemed to follow what Tone said. She took a step closer, as if to include them in a secret.

"Are you crazy?" she asked, so softly it was almost a whisper.

Ingrid looked at Erling, his head wobbled slightly.

"Are you mentally disabled then?" said Tone.

Neither of them replied this time either.

Ingrid howled softly. Erling shook his head, but he did that all the time, so it didn't mean anything.

"Are you Chinese?" said Tone, even more softly.

Ingrid turned and gazed at her with dark, impassive eyes.

"Are you Chinese?" Tone repeated. "You look Chinese."

At that point Ingrid opened her mouth, I saw her glistening tongue, I saw how her lips and tongue tried to form a word that perhaps was *yes*, perhaps was *no*, but sounded more like *thanks*; and that was when I first realized she could not talk.

Ingrid truly was not able to speak a word, even though she may have wanted to. But she could howl, softly and pleasantly, loudly and piercingly, perhaps almost evilly. When she howled it was as if something deep within her listened and understood what she meant. She could howl, and she could look at us with encouragement or acceptance, and somehow with love, as if she understood, or wanted us to understand.

I don't know how long we stood under the ash tree that winter day, at the spot that in reality was Matiassen's. An icy wind cut through to our bones. The thin ash tree branches looked like cracks in the clouds overhead, as if the sky were shattered and soon would tinkle down like broken glass. But the sky didn't fall. We stood there so Ingrid and Erling could see their new world: the rolling fields, the mountain ridges in the west, the edge of the forest, and the tall pine trees behind the house.

"Just think—you're going to live here with us!" Tone exclaimed enthusiastically, and then Erling began to laugh, while Ingrid howled softly and pleasantly.

Afterward we led Erling and Ingrid back through the snow. We walked in the wavering tracks we had made, up the steps and into the front hall, where we stamped the snow from our feet and took off our coats. Then we took Ingrid and Erling upstairs, knocked on the door, and delivered them across the threshold to Lilly.

7.

Every morning, spring, summer, and fall, Matiassen took his stool and tottered down the stairs and out to the ash tree. He would stand there several minutes before placing the stool exactly where it stood the day before, and the day before that. Every day the same, painful precision. When the stool was finally placed, he checked that all four legs rested firmly in the grass, and then he sat down with a kind of loving caution. It was as if there wasn't actually a stool under him, as if he sat down in midair and had to practice each day to believe the stool was really there. He sat down, placed his hands flat on his thighs, and began rocking his upper body back and forth, chewing his saliva constantly.

Every day the same routine.

I was the one who told Tone that Matiassen was crazy. One fall day I took her hand and led her toward the ash tree, until we stood several meters behind Matiassen's stool and saw him rocking.

"You see?" I said. "He's crazy."

Tone looked at me wide-eyed. Maybe she was afraid.

Matiassen sat there chewing his saliva so energetically you would think something was growing in his mouth, something that threatened to become too large, that was growing and wanted to get out, that he had to chew and chew in order to restrain it.

"Watch now," I whispered.

I let go of her hand, crept close to Matiassen, and stood directly behind him. The woolen blanket had slipped from his shoulders and lay on the ground; there were leaves in his lap.

"Hi," I said suddenly.

Matiassen did not react.

"Have you been in America?" I continued.

Matiassen chewed and chewed, without shifting his glance.

"Can't you talk?"

Still no answer. The stool creaked slightly. Leaves fell around us.

"Say something, you idiot!"

Matiassen sat exactly as before, rocked and chewed and paid no attention to me. I noticed that the four legs of the stool had made four deep cavities in the ground that were constantly getting deeper. The grass by his shoes was brown and trampled flat, and I saw that he had no shoelaces.

"Why don't you have any shoelaces?" I asked.

Matiassen did not reply.

I took a few quick steps forward. I don't remember what I had expected. Maybe I thought the rocking would stop, that he would spit out what was in his mouth, turn around, and talk to me. I lay my hand cautiously on his shoulder, and I would never have dared to do that if Tone had not been standing right behind me watching. My fingers touched the coarse material of his suit jacket, and he gave a tremendous start, as if I had touched him with a branding iron. Matiassen lost his balance, the stool tipped over, and he ended up lying in the grass. I was terrified and started to run. Tone followed me, and we ran all the way to the edge of the forest. At the stone fence we stopped and looked back. Matiassen had gotten to his feet, placed the stool in the four cavities, and sat under the tree as before. I still felt the coarse material of his suit jacket in my fingers; I had touched him, Matiassen had collapsed from the touch, and Tone and I no longer had any doubt that Matiassen was crazy.

It wasn't always like that. Matiassen had once been a railroad worker in America, and Christian Jensen had studied theology at the College of Wooster in Ohio. Matiassen and Jensen must have been among the most well-traveled in the entire parish. Both had crossed the Atlantic Ocean twice, they had seen two continents; both lost their sanity at some point; and both finally ended up in the room upstairs in our new house. Matiassen brought with him from America an old miner's lantern with two burners, and also a medal that was possibly pure silver. The lantern burned with a bluish, supernatural light, and we soon began using it when we went to the outhouse. Matiassen had worked on the railroad in the American West, and it was during that time that he lost his mind. It happened deep within a mountain: an explosive charge went off, parts of the tunnel collapsed, and several workers were trapped in total darkness. Matiassen was one of them. He never talked about the experience, but he had clippings from several American newspapers that reported the accident. Matiassen had been imprisoned for three days with a group of four men, and one of them—Mr. Edwards, who had worked in diamond mines in the Congo—told the *New York Herald Tribune* afterward that they could see nothing at all during those three days. But, he maintained, there was a reflection of light from the souls of the men that, after a while, began to gleam like the diamonds he once mined in the heart of Africa. Matiassen lost his sanity, but his soul had glittered faintly in the dark. After they were rescued, each of the four men received a medal for courage, and in the clipping from the *New York Herald Tribune* Matiassen stood with his medal beside Mr. Edwards and the two others. In the picture he looked much younger, but not especially happy or honored by the distinction, and I wondered if it really *was* Matiassen. It may have been someone else, but the medal for courage was the same. He brought it with him, along with the miner's lantern, when soon afterward he was sent by train across the prairie to New York, from there across the Atlantic, and then over the North Sea, until he finally ended up at Eg asylum in Kristiansand, where both the lantern and the medal for courage were taken away from him.

Everything was taken away from him, but nothing was thrown out. All his belongings were listed meticulously and stored in a secure place at the asylum, so when Mama and Papa took responsibility for Matiassen they also received his few possessions.

After Matiassen came to live with us, Josef somehow got permission to wear the medal for courage. I don't know how that happened; perhaps he asked to borrow it, perhaps he received tacit consent. In any case, Josef wore the medal very naturally, and with great dignity. He pinned it on his left lapel each Sunday before the church service, and then he sat and sang in the front row, on the right-hand side just below the pulpit, with the morning sun sparkling on the silver. Josef took charge of the medal and kept it so brilliantly polished you could see your reflection in it, and the rest of us shared the miner's lantern. So Matiassen's few possessions were useful to everyone. Josef wore the gleaming medal for courage, and the glow of the miner's lantern shone through cracks in the outhouse walls as if an angel of Our Lord had been revealed in the small cubicle above the manure cellar. Sometimes I saw the radiant light when I came out to the yard, and then there was nothing to do but turn around, go back into the house, and wait until the angel had gone.

8.

When Christian Jensen came to live with us he could walk almost normally, but could not hold a pen; his arms would suddenly fly up unexpectedly, and it had long been evident that he would never become a pastor.

Christian Jensen was originally from Mandal, and had been very gifted. Or *too* gifted, as people said. He lived with his mother, there was never any mention of a father, and early on it became clear that Christian would pursue a higher education. The plan was that after graduating from high school he would study theology in Oslo, but then unforeseen circumstances took him across the ocean to America. Some immigrant relatives wanted him to come, perhaps one of his father's sisters or perhaps his father himself. Nobody knew exactly. There was a school named the College of Wooster. Nobody knew where it was located either, at least not until he came to live with us and we saw the large brown envelopes postmarked Ohio. In any case, the college was apparently among the best in America, and the pastors trained there were said to have a special relationship with Our Lord. It was Christian's mother, Mina, who most strongly supported the idea of her son going to America. She told everyone how extremely bright Christian was. There was no end to the boy's talent—people said he had written an entire volume of poetry in just a few weeks, and the manuscript was being considered by Olaf Norlis Publishing Company in Oslo at the time Christian left on his long trip.

The poetry collection was never mentioned later.

Christian Jensen traveled alone across the Atlantic Ocean wearing his confirmation suit, and it was like going to the moon, or even farther. Back home in Mandal, Mina waited for a letter from her son. Weeks passed, but no letter arrived. Not until a college administrator wrote to say that Christian had been sick for a long time because he'd worked so hard at his studies. Later, another letter arrived saying her son suffered from a mysterious illness, perhaps the result of overexertion, which prevented him from holding a pen steady, so he couldn't write to her himself. The disease was called Saint Vitus' dance, but at the College of Wooster they believed the young Norwegian was losing his faith. He didn't stay long, and took no exams. However, he did have a special relationship with Our Lord.

He brought home a bundle of magazines from the college congregation, which had welcomed him warmly during the months he studied on the other side of the Atlantic. Later, when the war was over, large envelopes addressed to Mr. Christian Jensen arrived regularly at the rural post office in Vatneli. They were marked *Air Mail* and were plastered with stamps portraying American presidents. The envelopes came from the College of Wooster, were postmarked Ohio, and always contained new magazines from the congregation. Perhaps they thought there was still hope for Jensen, that there was a way back. In any case, he read the magazines thoroughly, and afterward his nightly conversations with Our Lord were intense. Tone and I would be awakened by his pacing. Slowly, stumbling a bit, he wandered back and forth, from the window to the stove, from the bed to the door, and over to the window again.

"Listen," Tone whispered. "He's speaking English."

And it was true, Jensen always spoke English when he talked with Our Lord. He said a few words, occasionally a question, occasionally a complaint, and then he seemed to listen to the answer he got before continuing in the same hushed way. In the morning he could sit quietly upstairs with the Wooster congregation magazine open on his lap as he pondered an idea that was somehow utterly bright and transparent, and at the same time dark and dangerously difficult. Sunlight streamed through the window that faced south and glided across his thighs while the idea took hold of him. Or he took hold of the idea. In any case, he got nowhere with it, not before the evening when he could talk with Our Lord again. Then at last he seemed to come alive. A guarded question. A trembling, indignant complaint. At times an almost forgiving tone. Afterward everything was quiet for several minutes, and in that stillness Our Lord answered him.

9.

One late winter day we went upstairs and got Ingrid and Erling and took them to the hayloft. The weather had become warmer, the sun shone above the forest and snow-covered fields, water trickled from the roof. The snow by the house had melted completely, the grass was brown, the earth dry. Matiassen had taken his stool outside and sat rocking in the sunshine wrapped in several layers of blankets. Suddenly Jensen appeared in the doorway. He stood on the top step for a long time. Thin, dressed in black, with a full beard, he looked like the picture of Jesus with a lamb and a shepherd's staff. The four of us stood watching him. Jensen waited awhile before he hobbled down the front steps, then he concentrated on holding on to the downspout at the corner of the house, and finally he let go of the wall and staggered across the yard toward the outhouse. It looked comical, and sometimes we laughed at him. But not that day.

"Come on, let's go upstairs," I whispered to the others. I don't know what I was thinking, but Ingrid, Erling, and Tone raised no objections. We hurried down the hayloft ramp and across the yard, splattering mud as we ran, and on our way up the front steps I heard Jensen fasten the hook on the outhouse door.

While the other three kept watch in the upstairs hall, I slowly pressed down the door handle. The air in Jensen's room smelled of old clothing and tobacco, medicines, ammonia, and possibly urine. There was nothing on the walls and the room looked bare, but the ceiling light was on, as it always was, even in the middle of the day when sunlight streamed through the windows. As I stole across the smooth floorboards, Tone and Erling stood in the doorway, with Ingrid right behind them vigorously licking her mouth. I walked as if on thin ice. The magazine from the College of Wooster lay open on the chair where Jensen usually sat. His neatly folded glasses lay on top of the magazine. I picked them up carefully, they were surprisingly heavy. Standing there holding the glasses, I had an urge to put them on to see if my eyes grew bigger, the way Jensen's did when he pushed them to the edge of his nose. But instead I picked up the magazine. It had long columns in small type, and everything was in English. Here and there I saw drawings and a few pictures, and I understood they were illustrations from the Bible, but also from a strange country that must be America, or perhaps hell. The pictures were full of terror and despair—faces contorted in pain and open hands raised toward a sky dark with thunderclouds. They were surrounded by devils no bigger than dogs, and floating in the air were dirty angels with huge, tattered, swanlike wings fluttering in the wind.

I stood there staring.

"Hurry up!" Tone whispered by the door. "Jensen is coming! Jensen is coming!"

But I just stood there. It was as if the pictures nailed me to the spot. Jensen was on his way, the door opened in the front hall downstairs, and soon I heard his clumsy footsteps coming up the stairs, but I just stood there, unable to move. The pictures burned themselves into me. I couldn't get rid of them. The faces, the devils, the angels. They swirled around me in the dark after we went to bed that night. Tone was asleep, I felt her even breathing on the back of my neck, but the pictures from the magazine did not let go. They never let go. The dancing devils. The dirty angels. I still see them.

10.

March came, April came. The frozen tower of feces and newspaper melted and collapsed in the outhouse. The ground was bare from the front steps all the way to the ash tree. Snowdrops sprouted by the hay barn and crocuses bloomed next to the house. Tone and I soon grew used to our new life with *the crazies from Stavanger*, as Josef called them. Mama hummed softly as she ran up and down the stairs with trays of food for Jensen and Matiassen, but we never heard her sing, not properly, not the way she had perhaps once dreamed of singing. Mama hummed while she sat on the milk stool in the cattle barn, her cheek against the cow's belly as streams of milk trickled into the pail; Papa hitched the horse to the wagon, slapped the reins, and the wagon rolled across the yard and disappeared down the road as he whistled a tune that had neither beginning nor end.

Each morning Tone and I walked two kilometers to the schoolhouse in Hønemyr. We started very early, before anyone upstairs was awake, except sometimes Josef, who would stand at the window watching us. Tone often went to school with me that winter, even though she was not yet five years old. We walked down to the milk platform, turned right and passed Jon and Tilla Båsland's house, and when we got a little beyond their hayloft we could glimpse Lake Djupesland lying white and still among the trees.

"Just think—when summer comes," said Tone, "we can go swimming!"

In the schoolroom we sat together at the very back by the window, and Nils Apesland stood in front by his desk as he directed our singing. He never sang himself, but he helped us keep time. Nils Apesland was a strange man. When spring came he walked across frozen lakes, even if the ice was melting, and if he met people he always said good-bye in case he broke through the ice and drowned. People had seen him in a white coat out in the fields at night performing some sort of religious ritual. They had heard him sing. Or perhaps it was a prayer. I sometimes thought that Nils Apesland could have lived upstairs with Josef, that he and Josef could have been brothers, were it not that Nils Apesland was so educated. He had gone to the teachers college in Notodden, where he was at the top of his class. Moreover, one Sunday he slid down Gaustatoppen Mountain on the soles of his shoes. He was extremely learned, and also wrote poetry, just as Jensen did before he lost his mind. The poems had been published in *Sennepskornet* magazine in Oslo, and when he finished teacher training Nils Apesland had walked all the way home to southern Norway. Almost no one had read the poems in *Sennepskornet*, but they were said to be about building your house on solid ground, and Nils Apesland had done that. His house stood next to an enormous scree, where he found grass snakes that he kept sort of as pets. The snakes came when he whistled, according to people who had seen it; he just squatted down and whistled a sad tune, and the snakes came wriggling out from the stones and ate butter from his hand.

The snakes *liked* butter. That wasn't just rumor. I saw the snakes myself. Nils Apesland stood at his desk; we had just sung a hymn, which he had directed as usual, when suddenly he pulled two grass snakes out of his jacket pocket.

"Don't believe people who say Satan looks like a snake," he said, holding up the snakes by their tails. "Those who say snakes are evil don't know the nature of snakes. Nothing is as kind and good and faithful as snakes."

He walked calmly among the students' desks with the two grass snakes so we could all see what he meant. The snakes wriggled up the front of his shirt and along his arms like flowing hat ribbons. They crawled up to the neckband of his shirt, then in and out of his beard, and when he went past our desk I saw the little tongues flicking against his throat.

Nils Apesland taught me to read, and during the spring Tone also began learning the alphabet. We sat on the firewood box in Josef's room in the afternoons while I helped her spell her way through the first pages in the reader. The flames in the small cast iron stove hissed and crackled; in the reader we saw pencil drawings of Henrik Wergeland's little horse, Veslebrunen, and of Wergeland on his deathbed. Tone thought he looked like Christian Jensen. I understood what she meant and had to laugh, but not loud enough to disturb Josef. He always had a tall stack of books on his night table; the Tower of Babel, he called it. Josef loved to read. Every Wednesday afternoon he rode to Brandsvoll on an old bicycle he had borrowed from Hans, or perhaps simply appropriated. He whizzed down the hill so fast the bicycle bell shook, past the milk platform and Sløgedal's house, across the Djupåna River, and on to the public library, which was in Dr. Rosenvold's waiting room. The entire book collection fit in two cabinets in one corner, and Josef began with A. He stood by the cabinet in the waiting room with his head cocked to the side, always on the lookout for new books, novels mostly. Afterward he rode home unsteadily with his string bag on the handlebars. He said he had read everything in the entire library; he had started from the beginning the fall he came to live with us. First Tryggve Andersen, then Bjørnson, then Dickens, then Dostoyevsky. But by the time he neared the end of the alphabet he had forgotten so much from the first books that he could just as well start from the beginning again.

11.

One day early in May Papa took all the children down to the roadside milk platform. Josef put on his uniform jacket and came with us. Nils walked in front with Josef and Papa, Tone held Ingrid's hand, Lilly carried Sverre in her arms, and I brought up the rear with Erling. When we got to the milk platform we waited there until the bus arrived. Josef drew himself up and saluted like an officer, his hand to his forehead. Erling and Ingrid moved closer to Lilly, Nils stood with his hands in his pockets, and Erling laughed and laughed at the big vehicle that had appeared from nowhere and stopped right in front of us.

The door opened and the driver shouted:

"So you're out giving them some fresh air! You should put them on a leash so they don't run away."

The passengers laughed. I didn't see who they were, I just heard the laughter. A few young people pounded on the windows, waved and shouted, and flattened their noses against the panes.

Papa's face hardened. He did not reply. Ingrid howled, and the driver shut the door again. The young people hammered on the windows even harder, but we all stood there without moving until the bus had driven away and everything was quiet. Then we walked home.

It was the second time they were compared to animals.

Shortly afterward we heard that the Germans had surrendered. Josef immediately got on his bicycle and rode to the Brandsvoll store, where others from the parish had gathered to hear the latest news from the outside world. There were rumors that Hitler had been arrested in Berlin, there were rumors that the Parliament building and the Royal Palace in Oslo had been set on fire. Joseph rode home, his lapels fluttering, as he shouted over his shoulder and tiny grains of sand pricked the bicycle's front fender.

A few days later there was a meeting in the Hønemyr schoolhouse, and we all went. That is to say: Jensen and Matiassen stayed home with Lilly and Sverre, but the rest of us left in the afternoon. The maps hanging in the schoolroom were unevenly rolled up, as usual. A ragged corner of North Africa, the mustard-yellow desert, the deep-orange Atlas Mountains. The blue Mediterranean, which became darker blue farther away from shore. Nils Apesland stood by the teacher's desk. Everything was as usual, except that the room was crowded with people. We barely found places at the very back by the window. More and more people came looking for information; they gathered outside, and finally the windows were opened so everyone could hear what was said. Nils Apesland related what he knew. It was true. Germany had surrendered. Adolf Hitler was dead in Berlin, Reich Commissar Terboven had blown himself up, Quisling had been arrested and was in jail at 19 Møllergata in Oslo. It was re ally true. At the end of his report, Nils Apesland said a short prayer. Sunlight fell obliquely through the windows, the dust sparkled, his face was brightly illuminated on one side, and I thought about the two wriggling snakes I had seen slipping in and out of his beard.

When Nils Apesland was finished, Josef suddenly rose from his chair.

"Since Germany has surrendered, would it perhaps be appropriate for me to sing a little song?" he asked.

All eyes turned toward him.

There wasn't a sound.

"Go ahead and sing, Josef!" someone shouted.

And that's what happened. Josef sang. Afterward he made a deep bow as the applause flowed over him.

Josef sang that evening too, at home in our living room. Everyone was there. Hans and Anna had come, Tone and I shared space on the bench at the end of the table, Jensen sat in a chair by the window looking very pale, his arms twitching nervously; Matiassen had placed his stool near the stove, Ingrid and her siblings had brought their chairs from upstairs and sat with us. It was the only time we were all gathered in the same room. Papa brought out bottles of mineral water, Mama served veal and salted kidney beans and steaming potatoes that had grown in a field with Virginia tobacco plants the past summer. Then we ate, and when everyone was finished, Josef stood up and tapped his fork against his glass.

"Snuff all the candles, and turn off the lamps," he said solemnly.

So Mama had to go around turning off the lamps and blowing out the candles she had just lit. Josef ordered that only one lamp be left on—the piano lamp. I sat on the floor next to Papa's chair and looked up at Uncle Josef expectantly.

"I'm going to sing some verses of a song," he began. "A song from the time I saw the midnight sun shining above the city of Trondheim. A song called 'Silver.'"

He straightened his uniform jacket and cleared his throat; the room was completely quiet, aside from the creaking of Matiassen's stool. Then Josef struck a key on the piano. It resounded deeply for a long time before Josef began to sing, and as always, he began at the opposite end of the scale. Josef sang with fine articulation, his voice was steady and confident, as though it had broken away from the rest of the strange, tall man. Usually he sang only during the worship service in church and on *the Big Day*—namely, his birthday, November 16—but he made an exception that day in May when freedom came. Josef sang, and I glanced at Tone, who sat with her eyes closed and her hands folded, as if she were praying.

12.

One morning Mama carried the kitchen chairs out to the yard and said we had to sit there in a row—Erling, Nils, Matiassen, Jensen, Sverre, and I—while Papa gave each of us a haircut. Papa had been the barber at Dikemark, he had cut hair for the mentally disabled and the insane, so he knew what he was doing. I sat there waiting for my turn while dry wisps of Erling's hair sprinkled onto his shoulders and drifted into my lap; Matiassen's tufts of hair fell heavily right to the ground, and when it was Jensen's turn, Mama had to hold his arms and upper body while Papa hurried to clip around his ears. Afterward we walked around with closely cropped heads, and I felt the cool breeze all the way to my skull. Then it was the girls' turn. Papa trimmed Ingrid's straight bangs, while Mama tied a red ribbon in Tone's hair and braided Lilly's. The only one who didn't want his hair cut was Josef.

"Remember Samson," he said. "Samson's strength lay in his hair!"

Josef went over to Tone, grasped her under her arms, lifted her onto his shoulders as she squealed with pleasure, and walked away with her.

"I refuse to give up my strength!" he shouted.

Ingrid and I followed him at once, and the four of us walked into the woods together. When I was younger Josef did the same with me: lifted me onto his shoulders and wandered away, often while talking to himself. Josef headed up a steep path with Tone enthroned on his shoulders. She laughed and sang and snatched at the lowest branches. It was easy to walk there, the path was firm and dry, and even if Josef didn't say anything, I knew where he was planning to go. Soon I saw the lake shimmering among the pine trees. I had been there many times before, sometimes alone, other times with Tone or Josef, but this was the first time Ingrid saw Lake Djupesland. The lake was surrounded by tall, dark pine trees on the northern side and broad, marshy areas on the southern side. During the summer, smooth water lily leaves grew up from the muddy bottom, and elusive white flowers opened on the water's surface. Twenty or thirty meters from shore a sandbar just barely emerged from the water, and sometimes in the summer a solitary bird perched there. I saw it myself once when I was with Josef. I was sitting on his shoulders, he paused abruptly, and the bird stood there motionless on one leg. I thought it knew something terrible that enabled it to stand like that. Something that was going to happen, or had happened. The bird knew it. Josef knew that the bird knew, and I understood that we needed to be quiet so it didn't become frightened and fly away.

Today there was no bird on the sandbar. Today only Tone's joyful shouts were heard in the forest. We trudged through marshland still frozen solid beneath our feet, then across rocky knolls, until the lake was in front of us. Chunks of milky ice lay close to shore, above us the wind sighed in the tall pines, and out on the lake, ripples suddenly appeared, and then disappeared just as quickly, as if someone had brushed a huge feather across the water's surface.

That was when I saw the dark spot spreading down Josef's back. Tone sat quietly on his shoulders, clearly afraid of what Josef would say. At first he seemed not to have noticed anything, he just looked out across the water; I said nothing either, I just stood behind him and saw what happened.

It would be the last time Josef dared to have any of us on his shoulders. Not even Samson's strength could have prevented Tone from piddling down his back while we stood gazing out at Lake Djupesland. Mama had to wash Josef's shirt and uniform jacket and Tone's pink dress. The clothes hung on the line when we went to bed that night, while Josef sat brooding in his room, and I lay for a long time listening to Tone's even breathing.

She would be the last.

13.

Everything happened at once. First five siblings from Stavanger arrived, then peace came, the birch leaves turned green, and we reached May 17, Constitution Day. The entire parish gathered to celebrate in the Brandsvoll meetinghouse, but despite their new haircuts, Jensen and Matiassen and all the siblings had to stay at home. The rest of us went to Brandsvoll—Josef on his bicycle, the others on foot or in the back of Hans's cart. At the meeting-house, all the radios and grain sacks the Germans had confiscated were cleared away, and the speaker's podium was pushed back to its place in front of the painting of the angel and the man with a hoe. There was room for nearly everyone in the building, and those who did not find space gathered outside. The windows were wide open, and people stood very quietly in order to hear everything that was said from the rostrum.

The pastor, Knud Tjomsland, who had been arrested the year before and had returned from Grini concentration camp, gave a short devotion. He was thinner, his voice was deeper, and he spoke more slowly than I remembered. When he finished speaking, he calmly stepped down from the rostrum and sat with the rest of us.

It was Tjomsland who had baptized Tone.

Mama sat with Tone on her lap, Josef sat beside her, erect as a soldier, and I gazed up at the painting of the man with a hoe. The poor fellow wore almost no clothes, just a cloth hung loosely around his waist; his face had a firm, determined expression, and one would think the simple hoe in his hands was all he owned in this world. I sat there looking at the man's anguished, heavenward gaze, his withdrawn yet gentle expression, and the angel, whom the man could not see. The angel was neither dirty nor damaged, but soft and shining like the light from Matiassen's lantern, and it hovered with open hands, as if holding an invisible child.

First the siblings from Stavanger, then the peace; Tone piddled down Josef's back, Tjomsland returned, and at the end of May both Lilly and Nils were sent to Kristiansand to be sterilized.

We understood that an important event was going to occur, but once the word was mentioned, it wasn't explained or discussed further. Lilly and Nils were taking an important trip to Kristiansand, and they would be away for several days. Lilly borrowed Mama's suitcase, which she packed for herself and Nils, and the day before their departure it stood in the front hall. When they were about to leave, we gathered in the yard—all the siblings, Josef, Tone, and I. Lilly said a few admonishing words to Erling and Sverre, Erling's head wobbled vigorously, Sverre clung to her skirt. The two younger brothers did not let her out of their sight, while Nils just stood with his hands in his pockets and grinned as if he owned the whole world.

"We're going away," Lilly said to the others. "And then we'll come back. And you mustn't cry."

Not a word from the younger siblings. No sound but the wind in the ash tree.

"You mustn't cry," Lilly repeated.

"No," said Nils firmly. "It's important." He stood next to Lilly and crossed his arms. "You mustn't cry."

It struck me again that Lilly was actually beautiful. Had it not been for the siblings, had it not been that she lived upstairs at our house, she would almost have been an ordinary woman with her own children and husband, a horse, and some cows in the barn, just like us. She stood there in a flowered dress with a narrow cloth belt around her waist, the wind caught her hair, swirling it in front of her eyes, and there was almost nothing that distinguished her from the other women in the parish.

Almost nothing.

Papa would take the bus to Kristiansand with Lilly and Nils, and then go with them to the hospital on Tordenskjoldsgata. He would leave them there, and stay at Hotel Bondeheimen until the next day. I don't know who had decided this. There was nothing in the contract. No letter from the Child Welfare office in Stavanger. Anyway. The decision was made. It would be a routine operation. Somewhat more complicated in Lilly's case, however. Nils would be first, then Lilly. It would hardly hurt.

We stood in the yard watching Papa, Nils, and Lilly walk down the road. Mama held Sverre in one arm and hung on to Erling's hand, while Ingrid clung to her skirt. When Lilly and Nils and Papa disappeared around the bend, Erling tore himself loose from Mama and ran after them. He raced along the hawthorn hedge as if fleeing his shadow, past Hans and Anna's house, howling and holding his hands over his ears. Then he disappeared from view, and we heard only his screams. Mama put Sverre down, gathered her skirt in her hand, and ran after Erling. I climbed up into the ash tree to see what was happening, and from there I saw Mama catch him. I saw Lilly, Nils, and Papa too. They had stopped down by the milk platform and stood there watching as Mama grabbed Erling and picked him up with his legs still running in the air. He shrieked and howled and waved his arms while Mama held him fast and carried him home. Soon afterward the bus appeared; it glided past the green fields, leaving a trail of dust, and stopped by the milk platform. Lilly, Nils, and Papa got aboard.

They were on their way.

Erling was still screaming when Mama carried him upstairs, with Ingrid at her heels. Afterward she came down to get Sverre, who hadn't moved during the whole incident and had dirtied his pants. Mama's face was drawn. She shut the front door sharply behind her, leaving Tone and me standing alone in the sunshine.

"Why is Erling screaming?" Tone asked.

"Because he's unhappy," I replied.

"Why is he unhappy?"

"Because Lilly and Nils are going to be sterilized."

"Why are they going to do that?"

"I don't know," I said.

I found a moss-covered branch from the ash tree, broke it in two, and threw the pieces far out into the field.

"Will they ever come back again?" Tone asked.

"Of course," I said.

"Will it hurt?"

"What do you mean?"

"To be sterilized."

"No," I said. "It will hardly hurt at all."

Erling kept on screaming even after the sun had gone down behind the hills in the west, and after a while Ingrid started a mournful howling. It was the first time I had heard her howl that way. A long, drawn-out wail that sank through the floor, and I thought it wasn't she who was howling, but something painful deep within her. The same thing that usually listened and understood. Now it howled in pain. She opened her mouth and it came out, filling the entire house until the walls almost split.

Mama stayed upstairs the whole evening. Tone and I were left to ourselves, as was Matiassen, who sat on his stool under the ash tree as twilight fell. Josef had sought refuge in his room long ago.

We stood by the window watching Matiassen rocking in the dusk, but then he must have realized it was time to come inside, because he suddenly got up, tucked his stool under his arm, and walked toward the house, like an ordinary working man on his way home from the forest.

We went to bed with the night-light on, while Erling and Ingrid continued to howl and scream on the floor above us.

"Aren't they going to stop soon?" Tone said.

"I don't know," I replied.

"Lilly and Nils are coming home again, after all."

"Yes, "I said. "But Erling is mentally disabled; maybe he thinks they've left for good."

We lay awake for a long time staring at the ceiling, and then suddenly everything grew quiet upstairs. I didn't know what had happened, but the screaming ended, the howling stopped; moths and night-flying insects circled silently around our night-light.

"Tell me a story," Tone said.

"What do you want to hear?"

"About the orange crate!" she exclaimed. "How it flew across the ocean."

"Okay," I said, and continued: "At one time the orange crate was full of oranges, and then it flew across the China Sea. Why it was able to fly, only the orange crate knew. It came first to Dikemark, and then Mama and Papa brought it here. First I slept in it, and later you slept in it. But the orange crate hasn't forgotten that it knows how to fly."

I paused. Tone looked at me. And at that moment we both heard it. The voice came from somewhere far away, as if from the forest or high above the house. Tone sat up in bed, wide-eyed.

"Listen," she whispered. "It's Mama. Mama is singing!"

14.

A few days later Lilly and Nils returned from the city. When Ingrid and Erling saw them they ran down the road toward the milk platform. Erling lost his shoes but continued in his stocking feet, waving his arms over his head; Ingrid howled and laughed a laugh that perhaps could not be called laughter. They met about halfway. Erling didn't know where to put his legs. Papa had to wrap his arms tightly around him until Erling calmed down, and then he walked the final stretch with us.

Lilly and Nils were home again. There was nothing different about them that you could see, they looked the same as when they left. Nils grinned, and Lilly was like a mother who had come home to her children.

"Have you been good?" she asked.

"Erling screamed and screamed," said Tone. "And Sverre dirtied his pants," she added.

Lilly looked at her.

"Is that true?"

"Absolutely true," said Tone.

A few seconds of silence followed, and nobody knew what would happen. Then Lilly seemed to soften, her whole face broke into a smile.

"We got Asina sodas at the hospital," she said.

They didn't tell us anything about what had happened. Not a word about the trip. Not a word about the hospital. Just about the bottles of Asina, and the corks that Nils still had in his pocket. Mama carried dinner up to them, all five were gathered around the table. They sang "Blessed Lord," and when the meal was over they licked their plates clean. Everything was the same as before. The new life could continue.

Everyone was allowed to smell the two corks before Nils collected them and lay down contentedly on his bed.

Not a word about whether it had hurt.

Everyone was home again, Mama no longer slept with the younger children upstairs; Tone and I lay in bed listening, but there wasn't a sound.

"Hear how quiet it is," said Tone.

"They've probably gone to bed."

"Tell me a story."

"What should I tell about?"

"About the orange crate! Tell the rest of the story about the orange crate."

"No," I said. "I don't feel like telling about that."

"Tell about Jensen and Matiassen then," said Tone.

"No," I said, rolling onto my side. "I've told you so much about them."

"Then tell another story," she persisted. "I want you to tell a story."

I lay peering into the room; behind me, I felt Tone sit up in bed.

"I could tell about the piano," I said.

"Yes! Tell about the piano!"

"You must never play Mama's piano," I began. "If anyone plays it, the house will rise and float away like an airship."

"That's not true," said Tone.

"I swear it's true," I replied.

Tone lay very still, waiting for more.

"Do you remember when Josef was going to sing?" I said. "He struck one key, and the whole house shook."

"I didn't feel that," said Tone.

"It's absolutely true," I continued. "If he'd played more, the house would have come loose from the foundation and we would have blown away with the wind, all of us."

"I don't believe you," said Tone.

"Don't you trust what I tell you?"

"No."

"Well," I replied, and closed my eyes, "it's true. Absolutely true."

15.

The crocuses by the house burst open—blue, and white, and yellow. Soon the Easter lilies were in full bloom, and their heavy flowers cast shadows that looked like sad old women. Then the tulips thrust through the ground, their petals unfurled, revealing the black faces inside.

One morning Lilly disappeared.

None of the siblings could explain what had happened. They were sitting around the table waiting when Mama brought breakfast upstairs, but Lilly's chair was empty, her bed was made, and her shoes were gone.

"Where's Lilly?" Mama asked.

The four looked at her.

"Not here, anyway," said Nils.

Papa quickly rode off on his bicycle and alerted neighbors all the way to Skinnsnes, and soon we heard that Lilly had been seen walking along the road past Sløgedal's house. She had looked purposeful and determined.

We all set out to hunt for her. Josef put on his uniform jacket with the medal on its lapel, Nils went with Papa, Ingrid and Erling came with the rest of us. We ran down the road and turned left by the milk platform, calling for Lilly.

Papa saw her first. We were only halfway to the store when he stopped and pointed.

"There she is."

Lilly stood knee-deep in the Djupåna River, out in the slow, dark current. We stayed up on the road, while Papa went down to the water's edge.

"So this is where you are, Lilly," he said. "We've been looking all over for you."

Lilly didn't say a word. She seemed almost ashamed, yet at the same time stubborn. When she saw us she squared her shoulders, looked at us coldly, and turned away as if in disgust.

"It's best you come ashore now, Lilly," Papa continued. "You could get sick, you know."

Lilly did not reply. The water flowed by silently. Now and then an eddy appeared and vanished. We sat on the bridge dangling our legs, waiting to see what would happen. Lilly just stood there with her arms held out to either side and her back to us, and it was impossible to tell what she was thinking. More and more people gathered around us on the road, and everyone stared at Lilly. Sløgedal rode up on his bicycle and stopped in the middle of the bridge.

"What's going on?" he asked.

"It's just Lilly," I replied.

Finally Papa sat down on a sandbank, calmly took off his shoes and socks, rolled his pants above his knees, and started wading toward her. River mud rippled like velvet around his white calves, the distance between him and Lilly became smaller and smaller. At last he was so close that he stretched out his hand to her.

"Come, Lilly," he said. "Just take my hand."

Lilly looked at the outstretched hand, and she looked at Papa. Then she started to wade out even farther. The water was now well up on Papa's thighs; he tried to grab her arm and pull her to shore, but she screamed and spit and shouted at him, until finally he had to let her be.

Lilly stood there in the river, her woolen dress rippling around her. Tone, Erling, Ingrid, and I were dangling our legs and sprinkling handfuls of gravel into the water when Mama arrived with Sverre in her arms. At first she was gentle and friendly, but firm. She turned to all the onlookers.

"Please go home now, all of you."

No one reacted.

"Everyone has to leave."

Nothing happened. Everybody just stood there. Sløgedal cleared his throat. Then someone at the back of the group laughed loudly.

"Do you hear me? Everyone has to leave. I need to be alone with her."

I heard mumbling and laughter, and people kept stopping on the road. That's when Mama exploded.

"Go home! Leave! Now!"

People seemed paralyzed. Mama had shouted so loudly the words echoed from the hills across the river. I sat there on the bridge and simply stared. Erling stared, Tone stared, Ingrid stared. Everyone stared at Mama. Even Lilly turned around in the river and looked at her aghast. Then, after a moment, Sløgedal fastened his pants clips, got on his bicycle, and rode toward the store without looking back. Others began leaving too, turned around as if by accident, spit in the ditch, put their hands into their pockets, and wandered away kicking pebbles and pinecones. Finally, everyone was gone. The road was deserted at last.

"You too," Mama said quietly, looking up at us. "You need to leave too."

We were at home when Mama and Lilly returned. I saw them walking arm in arm up the road from the milk platform. They looked like two girlfriends having a quiet, confidential conversation, or maybe like mother and daughter. When they reached our yard, Lilly kept her eyes on the ground while Mama looked straight ahead and didn't meet anyone's gaze. They walked past us and into the house, and nobody ever found out what Mama had said to Lilly.

People had seemed paralyzed, I'd sat on the bridge staring. But then Sløgedal had gotten on his bicycle, folks began to leave, and afterward, when Lilly came home again and sat at the table upstairs with her siblings, she was the same as ever. Lilly was the same, and Mama was the same. But I had heard. All of us had heard. Not only that Mama shouted, but that her shout echoed from the hills on the other side of the river.

It may have been after the river experience that Lilly became afraid of the water. She still felt that fear the day we drove along the seashore in Jæren and she lay in the car with her face in Ingrid's lap. Maybe the fear began when she realized she would never have children. Or it may have started later. Perhaps the time Josef took her to Lake Djupesland one summer evening many years later. The sun hung low in the west. They were gone a long time. Then we heard her screams, and soon afterward Josef came running home to get help. Lilly had started to scream as they stood by the water, he said, and he couldn't stop her. She screamed and screamed and refused to budge, until Papa slung her over his shoulder like a fireman and carried her home through the woods.

Maybe that's when her fear of water began. She and Josef had been looking out across the lake. Maybe he said something. Maybe a bird was hidden in the pine trees. Maybe he had touched her arm. I don't know.

16.

Several days after the incident with Lilly, Hans came to the door with two blind kittens he wanted to give us. He had found them in the hay the night before. Anna didn't want them, but Hans could not bear the thought of killing them, and so he thought of us. Josef immediately christened them Cain and Abel. For the first few days they lay in the orange crate under the woodstove in Josef's room. They licked drops of milk from his little finger, and he talked to them as if they were two babies. I'd been the first to lie in the orange crate, then Tone, and now Cain and Abel lay curled up there, dreaming of a world they had never seen.

Cain and Abel would later be immortalized.

One Sunday morning Nils Apesland rode up the road from the milk platform on his bicycle. Tone and Ingrid and I were standing by the hay barn with the kittens scampering around our feet when he entered the yard and waved to us. He had a black bag on his baggage carrier, and I thought there might be grass snakes in it, or his white coat. When Mama came out on the doorstep he asked if anyone in the family would like to be photographed. He had gotten a camera and was going around the area taking pictures of people, he said. Mama hesitated a moment, glanced at us, and then called to me.

Nils Apesland suggested we pose on the knoll just behind the hayloft, because the light was so pure there, he said. He told us to stand next to each other; Ingrid and Tone should hold Cain and Abel in their arms, I should be in the middle, and everyone should smile. Nils lined us up, and then took his camera out of the bag. It looked like a small accordion with a black bellows, but he didn't have a tripod like a real photographer. He got everything ready, while we waited patiently and Cain and Abel did their best to wriggle loose.

"Hold them tight," Nils commanded, and the girls held the kittens close so they couldn't get away. Then he stepped back slightly and raised his arm in the air.

"Don't move!" he shouted, even though all three of us already stood motionless staring into the camera.

"Now smile, everybody!"

And so the picture was taken.

It was sort of a sibling picture.

Ingrid to my right, Tone to my left, all of us smiling carefully. Tone and Ingrid each holding a kitten. The picture would later be sent to a painter in Oslo, Herbert Andersson. He would get specific instructions, but when it came to the kittens he could do as he wished. The photograph clearly shows that Tone and Ingrid are holding them tightly.

17.

Summer came. Swallows plunged from the sky like black lightning, Lilly's dress hung alone on the clothesline and danced in the wind. Tone and I were sitting on the knoll behind the house, about where Nils Apesland had taken the sibling picture, when the kitchen window opened; sunlight struck the glass as Mama came into view and called to me. When I entered the kitchen I saw she had made sandwiches for us, the bread knife lay on the cutting board, and she had poured pale currant juice into two empty milk bottles. Now she stood drying her hands on her apron.

"I thought we'd go swimming," she said.

"Swimming?"

Mama laughed, and rumpled my hair slightly.

"Why do you seem so surprised?" she said.

"Can we just leave?"

"Of course we can."

"What about Matiassen?"

"He'll be fine, I'm sure," Mama said. "After all, he just sits there."

"But what about Ingrid and Erling?" I asked.

"They can come along."

We walked single file along the path to Lake Djupesland, all five of us. Mama went first, carrying the sandwiches and clinking juice bottles, and the forest was fragrant with juniper and warm sunshine. We stood quiet as mice on the little bridge over the stream and peered down at a school of trout eerily moving to and fro in the current. The water was so clear we could see the yellow-green patterns that stretched along each fish and looked like old maps. Erling gleefully threw pebbles and dirt into the water, all the fish darted under the embankment, and we continued on our way.

Mama had changed recently. She walked ahead of us humming softly to herself, stopping now and then to bend branches aside, and when we were all sitting on the beach I thought she must be happy. Papa's eleven happy years truly had continued in the new house with Josef, Jensen, Matiassen, and the siblings from Stavanger, and now we all basked in the sunshine by the water and were happy together.

We sat with our feet in the coarse sand while we ate sandwiches and drank juice from the wide-rimmed milk bottles. The juice ran down the corners of Ingrid's mouth, she laughed and burped and got a big wet spot on her chest. A shallow inlet curved toward the east, and a forest of beach reeds rustled and bowed in the morning breeze. I was feeling full and sleepy from the food and sun, but then Mama stood up, brushed the sand off the back of her legs, and looked at us.

"Should we go for a dip?"

Mama held her arms out slightly from her hips as she waded

into the water. When it was well up her thighs she stopped, and I watched her surreptitiously. She wore only her underwear and her body was large and white; I'd never seen her like that before, at least not in daylight, and never under the open sky. The tips of the horsetails growing at the water's edge looked like the heads of huge matchsticks. Near the shore, tiny new broad-leaved pondweed sprouted from the water, while farther out on the lake, glossy water lily pads swayed with the slightest ripple. It was strange to see her like that. It felt like the night at Hotel Bondeheimen in Kristiansand when I lay next to her and felt her stomach against my back and her breath on my neck. I got up, brushed the sand off the back of my pants, and walked to the edge of the lake. I waded out a little, but stopped knee-deep in the water. Tone sat naked on the beach playing with pinecones, Erling thrashed the water with a branch nearby, and for a moment I caught the smell of mud and sun-warmed skin. Mama waded farther out, splashing water all around her; suddenly she leaned forward, or maybe she fell, water rushed against her breast and neck and she almost lost her breath, but soon she recovered, and calmly swam out toward the sandbar.

"Where are you going, Mama?" shouted Tone.

Mama turned onto her back and waved to us.

"Come on, children!" she shouted. "The water is wonderful!"

Suddenly a bird flew out of a tall pine tree on the other side of the lake. It had been perched there the whole time. Now it began a long, strangely silent flight just above the water's surface. Then it rose higher, soaring above the forest. It turned black against the sky, and then it was gone.

Mama hadn't seen anything. She swam steadily, with slow strokes, stretching herself, and I could see her tall, golden-white body as sunlight rippled over her back and hips. She headed toward the sandbar, and before long she reached it and could stand up, about forty meters from shore. Suddenly she was standing in water only ankle-deep. She was almost naked and not shy, and even though Ingrid and Erling stared at her, she just laughed and waved to us.

"Come on, come on, children!"

I'd never seen her like that before. She was thirty-six years old, something had changed. She stood on the sandbar and laughed, and it was like having her stomach against my back and feeling her breath on my neck.

I never saw her like that again.

18.

Her laughter echoed from the tall pine trees along the water. I could still hear it after we had gone to bed that evening. Tone was asleep. Her hair smelled like sunshine. A moth flew back and forth toward the ceiling, casting huge fluttering shadows.

The air was humid.

The next day the sky darkened. A mass of iron-blue clouds towered in the north, leaving the forest below in cool shadow. The birds stopped singing; only the bees still circled peacefully from flower to flower. From somewhere deep within the clouds came a dark, rumbling avalanche. Mama hurried across the yard carrying the zinc washtub and pulled the half-dry clothes from the line. As she stood there, the wind began to blow. Her skirt fluttered around her knees. A strong, cold wind came from somewhere far away, causing the lilac bushes to scrape against the house. Matiassen was still sitting on his stool under the ash tree when the first lightning slit the sky. His stooped figure became sharp and clear. Then a new, icy bolt of lightning slashed the clouds, and everything trembled in the sudden glare: the murmuring leaves of the ash tree, Matiassen's stool, and Matiassen himself. Next came a deafening clap of thunder, so loud the glasses in the kitchen cabinet rattled. Josef peered out his window, terrified. Ingrid, Tone, and I sought refuge in the front hall. Papa ran into the yard, lifted Matiassen off the stool, and carried him on his back into the house while the lilacs rustled violently in the wind. A new flash of lightning tore the heavens, the wall sockets crackled, and Lilly came running for refuge with us in the front hall. Then the rain began. Lightning and thunder followed on each other; Papa put Matiassen as far away from all outlets as possible, and I saw how the wild light flashed in Papa's eyes. The rain turned into a powerful hailstorm, pelting the windowpanes upstairs; water streamed over the gutters and knocked lilac leaves to the ground. Each flash of lightning struck a spot on the top of my head. It split my brain, ran down my spinal column, and tore me in two so quickly I almost didn't notice it. The thunder and lightning were like the picture of dancing devils and dirty angels in the Wooster magazine. I don't know how long the storm lasted, but it finally moved farther east. The time between flashes increased, but thunder still rumbled in the distance, like English bombers on their way across the sea.

Afterward the world was like new. Clean, shining, cool. The sun came out. Steam rose from the gravel, steam rose from the fields and the tree trunks behind the hay barn, steam rose from the barn wall itself. When Ingrid, Erling, Tone, and I went into the yard I noticed the curtains in Jensen and Matiassen's room were hanging out of the window and had become dark with rain. There were no bees, no birds. Mama's shoes stood at the bottom of the front steps filled with icy water. Everything was wet; water dripped from the trees, blades of grass glittered in the sun. Papa had put the four-wheeled horse cart by the hayloft where the yard sloped gently down toward the shed. During the last few days he had helped Hans haul sand for some concrete steps in the barn, but then the rain came and they had to wait for the sand to dry. He had turned the front wheels crosswise and placed stones by the back wheels so the cart would not move. There was a large box in the cart filled with sand that had become wet and heavy after all the rain. I climbed up and pressed my hand into the sand, leaving a clear imprint. Before long, Ingrid came and stood beside the cart; she kicked a wheel and tried to say something. I helped her up, and then Erling and Tone came too, but they climbed up by themselves. I made a handprint next to the first one, Tone made an imprint next to that, Ingrid and Erling just stared. My handprints looked like the tracks of a large, strange bird. Tone's prints were those of a slightly smaller bird. The two birds had wandered back and forth in all directions across the sand, as if looking for a place to build their nest. But then they had flown away.

"Look, Ingrid," said Tone eagerly. "Do it like this."

She took Ingrid's hand and pressed it into the sand, and after that Ingrid managed to do it by herself. We kept on for a long time, making a swarm of bird tracks in the wet sand, and in the end we were looking for the bird that had disappeared above the pine trees.

Then the cart tipped over.

For a moment it was as if I were flying; I flew, waving my arms, but surprisingly enough, landed on my feet. I heard the crash as the cart hit the ground. The box of sand fell over, and some sand spilled across the grass. I caught a glimpse of Ingrid's bewildered expression; the wind had been knocked out of her when she landed on her back. I heard Erling scream, but I didn't see Tone. She had suddenly disappeared. But then I saw one of her shoes under the wagon. And I realized what had happened. Tone lay with the cart partially on top of her; she didn't move, she didn't cry, and the silence made the blood freeze in my veins. I tried to lift the cart, but it would not budge. I shouted to Ingrid that she should run and get Papa, but she just lay on the ground gasping for breath.

I was underwater. Everything was quiet, or almost quiet; I heard a rushing sound bubbling around my ears. The bubbles rose and my heart pounded, and someone shouted my name, but the voice came from the depths beneath me.

Perhaps eight seconds went by.

At first Papa came walking calmly across the yard with wind-blown hair and his shirtsleeves rolled up. But then he must have seen a look on my face, or perhaps he saw Ingrid gasping for breath, because suddenly he began running. His shirt was open and flapped in the breeze. Hans arrived within minutes, and together they managed to lift the cart so Tone's back was free.

"Now, Tone," I shouted. "Now you can crawl out."

And she did.

She crept forward, perhaps as much as a meter, perhaps even farther—enough so that her back and legs were clear of the cart. And she was free. She was free, and there was blood on the ground, and in the grass, and on her dress. Erling screamed. Papa turned Tone over, her face was ashen. Her eyes were open and she gazed, as if astonished, at Papa and at Hans and at me, but then her eyes slid backward, her pupils disappeared, her eyes became white and empty, and Papa picked her up in his arms and raced toward the house with her feet dangling.

Mama was standing on the front steps when we came running. I saw her face stiffen. I saw how she dropped what she held in her hands, how everything just fell to the ground, limp and heavy. Her eyes, uncertain at first, abruptly grew frightened, and then darkened. Papa sprang up the steps with Tone in his arms, then ran through the front hall and into the bedroom, where he laid her on the bed. Ingrid and I stood in the front hall with no place to go. Josef was sent to get Dr. Rosenvold in Brandsvoll, and he rode off on his bicycle so fast the bicycle bell shook. I heard Mama's desperate voice in the bedroom, while Papa spoke calmly, and Hans tried to keep the door closed. Jensen tottered down the stairs, Lilly and Nils and Sverre followed, and I felt a terrible anger rise darkly from my stomach.

"Go back upstairs!" I shouted. "Go away!"

Jensen gave me a bewildered look through his glasses; for a moment I thought he would be furious, but he just made a little bow and hurried back to his room. Lilly took Nils by the arm and led him up the stairs, Sverre and Erling held hands and followed their big sister. Just then the bedroom door opened, Mama rushed out clutching her head and disappeared into the living room. She screamed, a flower vase fell to the floor, and I heard thundering tones from the piano. Then she slammed down the keyboard cover so hard the ominous sound reverberated long afterward. She came into the front hall again, and I didn't dare to look at her. I swallowed repeatedly, and Ingrid howled softly, softly, the way she did when she cried. Mama disappeared through the front door, out to the yard. I saw her down by the horse cart, which still lay overturned; she walked around frantically, as if looking for something she knew wasn't there. Then she disappeared into the hayloft. She screamed, she howled, and now and then she seemed to laugh a dark, unearthly laughter. Finally she ran toward the house, her face aflame. I held Ingrid's hand, deathly afraid of what would happen. Mama stormed right past us and into the bedroom. Through the open door I saw her lift Tone from the bed as Papa and Hans tried to stop her. Tone dangled in her arms, and Papa wanted her to leave; then she screamed again. The screams split the room apart. Everything cracked around us: the walls, the floor, the ceiling, finally even the sky above the ash tree outside.

"Karin!" Papa shouted. "Karin! Karin!"

He tried to take hold of her, but she stepped back, back, until she was standing against the wall. Papa put his arms around her, but Mama twisted out of his grasp. It looked as though they were fighting. It looked as if she hit him. Tone lay on the bed with her dress above her stomach, and one of her shoes lay on the floor in the front hall. Once again Papa tried to hold Mama, and this time he held her fast. He stood behind her, she threw back her head and let out a scream that pierced to the bone, but he held her tight, tight—so tight she could no longer scream, so tight he almost squeezed the breath out of her. Mama stood in his arms gasping for air, and then he loosened his hold. Slowly, slowly, until he held her no longer.

PART TWO

1.

In the fall of 1994 I cleared out the closet in Mama's bedroom. It was October, I was alone in the house. I had decided to start with the clothes. It was only her clothes; she had given away all of Papa's things after his death ten years earlier. There were blouses and sweaters, dresses, hats, and coats—clothes I hadn't seen for decades. Pantyhose, underwear, belts, and shoes. Her smell still lingered in the closet. It was in every piece of clothing; it gently surrounded me as I took the dresses off the hangers, folded them, and put everything neatly into black garbage bags. By the time I came to the bottom shelf in the closet I had five full bags standing in the upstairs hall.

The bottom shelf was full of shawls, mittens, leather gloves. They were an entire armful, and I started filling a new garbage bag. When I turned back to the shelf, I discovered a plastic bag that had been hidden under everything else. I had no idea what was in it; I stood with the bag in my hands for a moment, then emptied its contents onto the bed. It was Tone's clothes. I recognized them immediately, even though I hadn't seen them for almost fifty years. How could that be? I thought everything had been burned. But there was no doubt about it. This was her yellow sweater with the loose buttons and her pink wool dress, and these were her little brown woolen stockings. The sight of the small clothes hit me harder than the smell of Mama. I had to take a break. I went out into the yard without a jacket, and stood there until I began to feel cold. The leaves on the ash tree were still green, but much lighter than during the summer, as if the green was on its way back into the tree, into the branches, into the soil. The clothes must have lain there the whole time. A whole life. I took a few deep breaths, then went upstairs again. The little dress smelled faintly of mildew and wood. Although the garments had surely been washed and ironed and folded nicely, they still seemed dirty. The zipper was rusty. The stockings had holes in them. But everything was there. Everything, everything.

I took the wool dress down into the living room and over to the painting that still hung above the piano, and I saw that, yes, it was true. It was the same dress. That was a strange moment. I felt as if time itself opened up and gaped at me forebodingly. I stared at the painting and Tone gazed at me with that gentle smile of hers as she clung to the kitten.

Herbert Andersson had clearly not followed the strict instructions he received. After he finished the painting, he sent the clothes back, and Mama had not burned them when they were returned from Oslo. She had saved everything. For almost fifty years they had lain neatly folded, ready to be worn, while the little zipper rusted. Mama must have known that I would be the one to find them. Nothing had been thrown away. Everything was there, except for the red hair ribbon.

2.

When Dr. Rosenvold finally arrived, Papa was standing in the front hall, completely stunned. The knees of his trousers were covered with sand and his shoes made a crunching sound when he accompanied the doctor into the bedroom. Mama was sitting on the bed; she didn't make a sound, just rocked her upper body back and forth. Tone's shoe lay on the floor in the front hall. I grabbed Ingrid's arm, and we ran out into the yard and down behind the hay barn. I threw myself on the grass, which was still wet after the rain, but Ingrid kept standing until I ordered her to lie down too.

"Come here, Ingrid," I said. "Lie down. We need to pray."

Ingrid merely stared. Her eyes were dark and narrowed, her hair tousled as usual. She just stood there, and I shouted to her again.

"You need to pray," I hissed. "Do you hear me, Ingrid? You need to pray!"

Soon afterward Anna and Tilla came running across the yard and disappeared into the house. I heard their voices, but then everything grew quiet inside. Absolutely quiet. The front door banged in the wind. Before long Josef appeared, but he didn't run. He paced back and forth on the front steps with his hands in his jacket pockets, as if waiting for someone. But nobody came, and finally he went inside again. I heard Mama's voice far away and covered my ears. After a while Anna came out on the front steps with Papa. She held Papa's arm tightly. It looked as though he was going to fall, but he didn't. They went down a few steps, then they stopped, and Papa held on to the railing. He ran his hand over his face a few times, as if trying to tear it off, and then he called to me; he called my name several times, while Anna held on to him. Ingrid and I lay absolutely still. I didn't have to order her, suddenly she seemed to understand. She folded her hands so tightly her knuckles turned white, and I did the same; I prayed with my face in the grass and breathed the smell of the earth.

We lay there for a long time. I heard the wind in the ash tree. The bees buzzing in the lilac bushes.

Finally, Hans came and found us.

I didn't hear him until all of a sudden he stood in front of us with shiny wet boots. I don't remember what he said, and I don't remember what I replied. I remember only his voice, deep and slow and ordinary. Ingrid was sent upstairs to Lilly and the siblings, and Hans carried me down to Anna's kitchen. I could have walked on my own, but Hans carried me anyway. He grasped me around the waist and picked me up. It was strange and unusual, but I didn't object, and Hans didn't say anything. I heard his breathing and his boots rhythmically brushing against his calves. He smelled of horses, of earth, of hard work. I wanted him to talk to me, but he didn't say a word, and before long I felt listless and indifferent to everything. I must have closed my eyes, because I don't remember anything else until we were in Anna's kitchen. Everything was quiet and peaceful there, as it usually was. Hans set me down on the kitchen floor, and disappeared out the door. Anna fixed some food for me; she buttered slices of bread and poured milk into a glass, talking all the while about small, everyday things as if nothing had happened.

"Where is Tone?" I asked when she put the bread on the table.

"We're not going to think about that," said Anna.

"She crawled out after all," I said. "I told her to crawl out, and she did."

Anna looked at me. Her silence was gentle and loving and without mercy.

"She heard me," I said.

Anna did not reply.

3.

I stood by a body of water. Perhaps it was Lake Djupesland, perhaps it was the sea. Perhaps it was summer. Josef wasn't there, Tone wasn't there, nor were Ingrid or Erling. I stood alone. Ahead of me, the sandbar was barely visible above the water's surface. No bird was perched out there, perhaps it was hidden in the tall pine trees. I felt an incredible urge to wade out and start swimming. But something prevented me. What it was, I couldn't say.

Then I woke up alone in bed.

Mama sat on the piano bench in the living room. The room was light and white and quiet. No one shouted, no one screamed; the crunch of sand was no longer heard in the front hall. Tone's shoe was gone, and Mama sat calmly staring into the air with her hands in her lap.

Josef stood by the piano in his uniform jacket, as if he was about to strike a key and start singing, but he didn't sing. The sexton, Reinert Sløgedal, had arrived, Hans and Anna stood by the door, the sheriff, Kristen Lauvsland, sat at the table writing on a piece of paper. The only sound came from the sheriff's pen; sunlight streamed through the window, and I saw the shadow of the sheriff's hand as he wrote.

It was a warm, brilliant day.

All the patients, except for Josef, were locked in upstairs. Matiassen's stool stood under the ash tree, but there was no sign of Matiassen. Cain and Abel were chasing each other around the legs of the stool, and I wanted to go and sit in his place. I thought about the faint glow from the trapped souls in the railroad tunnel that had collapsed somewhere in America. The stool stood there empty; I wanted to see the same things Matiassen had seen, but I didn't go outside and sit down. I just stared out the living room windows while the swallows flew so high they almost disappeared against the sky. Sløgedal cautiously cleared his throat; the sheriff got to his feet, his chair scraped the floor, and he held out a piece of paper to Papa.

"Here," said the sheriff. "This is for you."

The paper drooped in the air before Papa took it.

A black car was parked in the yard. Sunlight shone harshly on the hood. The wind sent a pale green sigh through the pine forest, velvet grass billowed in the fields, yarrow quivered in the ditch. My stomach ached. The sheriff went out to the front steps, and Josef followed at his heels. They crossed the yard slowly and walked with Sløgedal, Hans, and Papa down to the horse cart, which nobody had touched yet. They stood there for a long time, and I saw how Josef always took care to stand next to the sheriff. I didn't hear what they said; the wind took away their words.

I found the spot where Ingrid and I had lain in the grass, and I lay there a long time waiting for someone to come and find me.

Eventually I must have fallen asleep, because when I woke up I heard voices nearby. Josef and Papa stood next to the sheriff's car, while Sløgedal took off his hat and seated himself on the passenger side. Josef raised his hand smartly to his forehead as the sheriff got behind the wheel. The engine started, and they drove away.

I kept lying in the grass while Papa and Hans went back to the cart. They managed to get the box of sand out, but it required all their strength. First they spent a long time digging out the sand, and then they tipped the cart back up on its wheels with a crash. I lay very still and caught a glimpse of Papa through a mass of waving grasses and flowers. The two men didn't say a word. All I heard was the rasp of spades in the sand. Finally, Hans harnessed the horse and left with the cart. I closed my eyes and pressed my face into the grass. The sound of the cart wheels was like four millstones that ground everything beneath them to dust. When I glanced up I saw Papa standing alone. He just stood there, the way he had stood on the front steps with Anna. Again he rubbed his hand up and down his face. Then he rammed the spade into the ground. It didn't stay upright, but he didn't bother to pick it up. He started to walk toward the house. I was afraid of what would happen if he suddenly discovered me. He wouldn't recognize me, I thought. He would chase me away. Or scream. Papa walked past without seeing me and continued almost to the front steps. Suddenly he stopped. He paused under the ash tree for a moment, next to Matiassen's stool. Then he called me. Once. Twice. His voice was strange and distant, and he seemed to hear that himself, because he didn't call anymore. I pressed my face into the flattened grass. Everything grew quiet. Just the sound of the wind, the lilacs scraping against the house, and the cheerful shrieks of the swallows as they swooped down from the sky. When I looked up, Papa was no longer there, but Matiassen's stool was gone. I got to my knees, and then I saw Ingrid in the upstairs window. She stood motionless, peering down at me. Her face was white and indistinct, but it was Ingrid. She had been watching me the whole time. I waved slightly. And instantly, she disappeared into the darkness.

4.

I couldn't get rid of the sight of Mama. I couldn't get rid of the sight of Papa holding her tightly. It was like the devils and the dirty angels. Images of Mama and Papa danced around me in the dark. The night smelled of wet, new-mown grass; mowers were out in the fields before the birds began singing. I slept lightly. I glided like strange, deformed air bubbles under the ice, and awoke before sunrise. I lay very still under my duvet, as if a blanket of snow lay on my chest, and I heard bees buzzing peacefully outside the window. Everything blossomed, and the bees flew through the evenings as if they carried the weight of their dreams on their backs.

Mama was suddenly calm.

Even so, I didn't dare to look at her. She was completely calm, but seemed blind and deaf to everything that happened around her. I saw the bird that flew low over the lake before it suddenly rose above the forest. I heard the echo of laughter from the pine trees on the other side of Lake Djupesland.

Later, Knud Tjomsland arrived.

We heard the car approach, and I watched through the window with Lilly, Nils, Sverre, Erling, and Ingrid as the pastor got out of the car, closed the door behind him, and walked across the yard. When he knocked on the door downstairs, we all looked at one another. We listened, quiet as mice, and heard Tjomsland enter the front hall. We heard Papa's voice and the pastor's voice, which was deep and deliberate, the same as it had been in the meetinghouse. After that, heavy footsteps moved across the floor and into the living room, the door shut, the voices grew softer and faded away.

"Yeah, yeah, by George," said Nils, and lay down on his bed.

The pastor remained for perhaps an hour and I stayed upstairs with the siblings; the whole time Nils kept running his fingers slowly through his hair. When we realized Tjomsland was leaving, Ingrid and I ran to the window. Josef stood in the yard ready to accompany the pastor to his car. He held the car door open for him, and I saw their shadows almost merge. Tjomsland said a few words to Josef and gave him a friendly clap on the shoulder, Josef raised his hand in a salute, the car disappeared down the road, and Josef was left standing alone.

The next day I was awakened by cautious footsteps on the stairs and lay blinking in the gray morning light. It wasn't Mama or Papa, not Jensen, not Matiassen, and not Josef either. I was wide awake at once, and sat up in bed.

"Tone," I whispered.

Later, when I opened my door, Josef stood by the mirror in the front hall wearing his uniform jacket and smoothing his mustache with a shoe brush.

"Today you and I are going out in the world," he said, taking my hand.

The door to the living room was closed. There wasn't a sound, but I knew Mama and Papa were in there, and I understood that they wanted to be alone.

Josef and I wandered aimlessly in the yard while Cain and Abel scampered around our feet. Matiassen's place was empty, the stool wasn't there, but I saw the four deep cavities from the legs, and the grass was completely flat in a circle around them. As we stood there, Papa came out on the front steps and called to us. Cain and Abel were fighting with my shoelaces. Josef took my hand, and though he didn't say anything, I knew what was coming.

The door to the living room was open, but when we were about to cross the threshold, Josef hesitated. It was like the time Tone came to this earth; Josef and I were at St. Josef's hospital in Kristiansand, and neither of us wanted to be the one who took the first step into the room. Now too, we were coming to see Tone. The coffin rested on two kitchen chairs in the middle of the room, and I smelled the heavy, sweet scent of flowers. Mama was sitting on the piano bench, but she stood up when we arrived and almost disappeared in the sharp light from the windows.

"Just come in," said Papa.

Josef did not budge. I tugged his hand, but his whole body had become stiff as a board.

"Come on, Josef," I said.

Josef shook his head. I tugged and pulled, but he didn't move. Finally, I let go of his hand and walked across the room alone.

Tone lay there as if she were asleep, but her face had changed. She looked older. Her lips were almost the same color as her skin and sort of melted into her cheeks. Her hair was darker and longer, her nose more pointed, her mouth half-open, like when she skipped across the grass. I heard the clock ticking on the wall. I looked at the folded hands and the bouquet of carnations, and in a way it was Tone lying there, but at the same time it wasn't. Papa came and put his hand on my shoulder. The light, almost unnoticeable touch made something well up in me. I twisted myself loose and took a few steps back; I saw Mama look at me, she moved toward me slowly, but I didn't meet her eyes. I turned to Josef, who was still standing in the doorway, and at that moment he seemed to take courage. He hurried across the room, took my hand firmly, and led me out of the living room, through the front hall, out onto the front steps. He led me into the yard and didn't let go of my hand until we reached the shade of the ash tree. After that I began running, and only then did I start to cry.

5.

My stomach ached, high up, about where my rib cage ended. It was worst in the evening. Out of habit, I lay toward the edge of the bed so Tone would have space next to the wall. I lay there for a long time listening for her breathing. Finally I fell asleep, but awoke in the middle of the night because she wasn't there. I smelled the scent of carnations.

The funeral was on a Friday.

Mama had laid out my best clothes on the bed. I took a long time; I stood by the window and watched the swallows while I buttoned my shirt, and when I finished dressing Papa squatted in front of me and combed my hair with a comb dipped in sugar water. I gazed at the knot in his tie, and he didn't say a word. My hair became stiff, and it felt as if I were wearing a helmet. My shoes creaked when we stood in the front hall.

"Where are Ingrid and Erling?" I asked.

"Upstairs," said Papa.

"I want Ingrid and Erling to come with us."

"Ingrid and Erling are going to stay here," said Papa.

"I want Jensen and Matiassen to come with us," I said.

"They're going to stay here," Papa said brusquely.

"Why?"

"They can't come along."

"Why not?"

He didn't answer.

"Who's going to take care of them?"

"Today they have to take care of themselves," said Papa.

As he stood in front of the mirror combing his hair back smoothly, he was very calm. He looked almost like the wedding picture where he had his hands behind his back. He put the comb in his pocket and straightened his tie, then he took my hand and we went out to the yard where Mama, Josef, and Anna were waiting in the shade.

Josef was the only one from upstairs at the funeral.

I sat next to him in the front row, close to the baptismal font. Josef sang loudly and impressively, while I looked up at the painting of the Ascension, the gilded acanthus vines, and the eye of God staring at us from a shining triangle at the very top. God gazed down at us coldly, and Josef sang "Joyful, Joyful Each Soul That Has Peace." The swallows were flying back and forth from the church tower when we came out into the sunshine, the bell swung in the dark tower, and I saw the weather vane that always pointed north. Papa and Hans carried the coffin with Sløgedal and the sheriff. Mama followed them, and was very calm. I walked beside her, staring at the ground; our shadows stretched ahead of us in the grass, and I didn't want them to merge. I walked silently beside her and guarded my shadow. I waited for her to suddenly let out a terrible scream, so Papa would have to hold her tight. But that didn't happen. Mama walked calmly, and I kept our shadows apart. We walked to the open grave, and Mama stood as if turned to stone while Tjomsland sang, his voice almost swept away by the summer breeze. Tjomsland sang, and the swallows flew to and from their nests. Then we all sang, and the one who sang loudest was Josef, standing shoulder to shoulder with the sheriff. I heard Josef sing and looked over at Mama, but I didn't see her face. I didn't remember her face. It had disappeared. But I knew it was Mama standing there. Her dark, quiet form. And her shadow that stretched almost to my feet.

6.

The night smelled of earth and white carnations. Everything was quiet. A paralyzing stillness fell on us like snow. The siblings' tin plates no longer clattered upstairs, Josef lay on his bed in his room reading silently, Matiassen no longer sat outside on his stool. Jensen had even stopped his nightly conversations with Our Lord.

Everyone had become quiet. But Mama laughed in my head.

I knocked on the siblings' door. I heard footsteps approaching, the door opened, and Lilly stood there looking at me.

"What do you want?" she said.

"Can I come in?"

Lilly hesitated, but then stepped aside and let me in. The table was set, the four others sat on their chairs looking at me.

"What does he want?" said Nils.

"He didn't say," Lilly replied.

"I just wanted to say hi," I said.

"Hi," muttered Erling, his head wobbling.

"We're going to eat now," said Lilly.

"Okay, I'll leave," I said.

Ingrid regarded me silently with gentle eyes. Then I hurried downstairs before Papa brought up the food.

School began in the fall, and I walked the two kilometers alone. I sat alone at the desk farthest back in the classroom while Nils Apesland stood at the front and directed the singing. I saw the maps rolled down behind him, the Atlas Mountains and the Mediterranean Sea, which got deeper and deeper the farther you went from the shore. Each morning I walked down the road alone. I knew that Ingrid and Erling were standing by the window upstairs and saw me leave. I knew if I turned around they would immediately hide behind the curtains. But I didn't turn around. I just walked to the Hønemyr schoolhouse and sat at my desk looking out at the forest and the sky while everyone sang.

I went upstairs alone and knocked on the siblings' door. Each time it was Lilly who opened it, each time she gave me a suspicious look, but each time she let me in. I stayed with them for a few hours in the afternoon. Nils lay on his back in his bed pensively running his fingers through his hair, Sverre played on the floor, Ingrid and I sat at the table while she watched me draw. I stayed until they were ready to eat. The same bickering when the food was put on the table, the same howling and hullabaloo that I'd heard only through the floor before, and then "Blessed Lord," which they always sang. I sang too. Nils sang with a childlike voice. Ingrid howled softly, while Lilly kept her eyes intently on me. I heard my own voice clearly.

In the evenings Papa sat by himself in the living room smoking the last of the Virginia tobacco that remained after the war—tobacco that he had said was only for special occasions. I didn't know where Mama was, but I knew Papa sat there alone. I lay in bed without moving, and in my mind I pictured the smoke curling from his mouth. I imagined him surrounded by a spirit that came if you rubbed a lamp for a long time, but the spirit could not help him, it could not fulfill any of his wishes. Nor could it help me or Mama, or fulfill any of our wishes. Only then did I realize that time had stopped.

Time stopped the day the cart tipped over, but still the weeks slipped by. The days were short and mild, with quiet sunlight from morning till evening. Rose hips ripened along the stone fences, blackbirds pecked the soil under the hawthorn hedge, swallows gathered in long, disorderly rows on the electric wires, strangely silent. They sat close together, as if watching each other, as if none wanted to be the first to fly.

One day they were all gone.

One morning the grass was white with frost, one morning the puddles were covered with a thin film of ice that cracked under my feet, and the next day the yellow leaves of the aspen trees loosened as they rustled in the wind.

I had a dream. I dreamed about the orange crate, which was on its way across the China Sea, floating perhaps ten meters above the water. It kept floating, and the sea was endless and beautiful and glittering, until I saw that Tone lay in the orange crate holding white carnations. I awoke with a start, and the dream didn't leave me until I'd eaten and washed my face and was on my way to school in the dusky morning light.

Long, gray days of rain arrived.

I knocked on the siblings' door.

"Can Ingrid come outside?" I asked when Lilly opened the door.

"No," said Lilly. "It's raining. Ingrid can only go out when it's sunny."

I kept standing in the doorway.

"Then can I come in?" I asked.

"Okay," she said. She let me in and shut the door, and I stayed there until Papa came up to get me that evening.

I lay in bed and heard Mama and Papa talking softly in the living room. It was Mama's voice I heard; Papa only made comments that didn't need many words. After a while she rose, walked across the room, and slammed the door. I could tell that she stood for a moment in the front hall, perhaps she looked toward the door of the little room where I lay, perhaps she wondered if I was asleep. I closed my eyes and heard her take her coat from the row of coat hooks and then sit down on the chair by the mirror to put on her shoes. Next I heard the front door open, and then Mama disappeared into the night. I lay in bed and sensed how quiet everything became when she left. Through the half-open window I heard her quick footsteps going down the road; they grew more and more distant, and finally faded away completely.

I understood that something had happened. A few days later Mama's suitcase was in the front hall, the same suitcase she used when we left Drengsrud and when she traveled alone to Kristiansand when Tone was born. The suitcase was there when I came from school. No one said anything, but I realized something had happened. Papa was upstairs with Jensen and Matiassen, Mama was in the kitchen. I went upstairs and knocked on the siblings' door.

Everything was quiet during the evening.

The house lay under a starry sky and I listened for footsteps, for voices. But no one spoke, no one walked across the floor. Mama and Papa sat together in the living room, but they didn't say a word. I realized that Mama was going away, her suitcase was packed, but I hadn't dared to ask where she was going.

The next day the yard lay in tranquil autumn sunlight, the hay barn cast sharp shadows toward the west, the leaves on the ash tree had lost their color, and a gentle breeze turned the edge of the woods into trickling gold.

Papa carried the suitcase outside and set it down at the bottom of the front steps. Hans and Anna strolled through the garden and stopped by the hawthorn hedge. Mama knelt in front of me; she buttoned the two top buttons on my jacket, then changed her mind and unbuttoned the top one, moistened a finger with saliva, and rubbed away a spot on the arm.

"You must be good to Josef," she said.

I nodded.

"And keep an eye on Ingrid and the others," she continued.

I nodded again.

"Promise me?"

"Yes," I said.

Then she stood up, gave me a light, absentminded pat on the head, and turned to look at Papa, but I didn't see her face.

"You can come with me down to the milk platform if you wish," she said to the siblings.

And that's what happened.

Mama and Papa went first, then Erling, who tramped so hard the dust rose from his shoes, next came Nils with his hands in his pockets, Lilly led Sverre by the hand, and Ingrid and I brought up the rear.

"Greet the king for me!" Josef shouted from his window upstairs.

As we passed the hawthorn hedge Hans raised his hand to us, and Anna clutched her sweater more tightly around her.

When we got to the milk platform, Papa set down the suit-case in the gravel and rubbed his hand up and down over his face the way he had on the front steps. We all stood looking at him. I waited for him to say something, or for Mama to say something, but nothing was said—not until we heard the hum of a vehicle in the distance and the bus came into view. Then Ingrid began a soft, restrained howling. I took her hand and she quieted down. We all watched as the bus slowed and finally stopped in front of us. There was a warm smell of diesel as the engine idled, and the shaking made the windows rattle. I saw people sitting inside, but I didn't know any of them. It was the same driver who had shouted at us the day Papa's face hardened, but now there were no youngsters pressing their noses against the windowpanes, and this time the driver didn't say a word. Papa picked up the suitcase and went on the bus with Mama. The two of them stood between the rows of seats for a moment, but I didn't see their faces, just their chests and part of their arms. Then Papa turned around and stepped down from the running board empty-handed. The bus started with a jolt, and we watched it disappear around the bend in the road.

7.

I thought maybe she would come back the next day. I thought maybe she spent the night at Hotel Bondeheimen, that she slept in the same room where I'd heard the sounds of the city and felt her stomach against my back. I lay in my bed while Papa took care of Jensen and Matiassen upstairs, I heard his voice and footsteps crossing the floor, and I heard the commotion from the other end of the hall as Lilly put the siblings to bed. Finally everything was quiet.

Mama did not return.

I thought maybe she would come the following day, but she didn't. That afternoon I saw the bus, but it didn't stop at the milk platform, it just continued on, with hardly a sound.

The Virginia tobacco was gone.

Lying in bed at night, I smelled the scent of carnations. I heard the British bombers roaring in from the sea in the southwest, I heard the metal machines flying high above the clouds and the forest and the house.

Then suddenly I remembered the war was over.

I remembered the time Tone was born. Everything Mama had told me.

Mama had traveled alone to Kristiansand, to St. Josef's hospital, not far from the Aladdin cinema. Through gaps in the blackout curtains she had seen the sky and the clouds drifting in from the sea. In the evening the baby was brought to her. The little girl had been bathed and fed and lay quietly in her arms while Mama heard the German soldiers come out after the last showing at the Aladdin. The soldiers walked past the hospital windows in a cheerful mood and their shadows flowed together on the ceiling above her. The men continued across town, and when they were far away, Mama heard them singing. Soon there were only the scattered sounds of the city, and then the rain came in from the sea in the southwest.

I lay in the dark and pictured everything in my mind.

Later, someone carefully picked up the little girl without waking her, and rolled her into the nursery where the other newborns were sleeping. The light was turned off; Mama lay alone in bed, drew the blankets around her, and listened to the sound of the rain. It was impossible to sleep. She lay awake the whole night. The wind and rain intensified, and now and then she heard babies crying somewhere far away, but it was not her baby.

She was absolutely sure. It was not her baby.

I remembered the day Papa and Josef and I went to get Mama and Tone at the hospital, while Anna and Hans cared for Matiassen and Jensen. Josef stood in the front hall in his well-worn uniform jacket and fastened Matiassen's shiny, newly polished medal on his lapel. He had his Border Resident card in his pocket, and smoothed his bristly mustache with a shoe brush.

I remembered the corridors at St. Josef's hospital, and how Mama had to coax Josef and me over to the hospital bed.

"Come and see your sister," she said encouragingly.

But I didn't want to do that. Josef seemed anxious; I held his hand, but neither of us dared to take the first step.

"She already has a name," Mama continued. "Her name is Tone."

"Tone?" said Josef.

"Tone?" I repeated.

"Yes," said Mama. "Isn't that a nice name?"

I drew Josef across the room to Mama, and then we both saw the small creature lying in her arms. It was the first time I saw Tone, the date was September 15, 1940, and in the hospital garden, the wind surged through the elm trees like huge waves. That was the day I saw the ocean for the second time.

I didn't remember anything about the trip back home, but I remembered the lights were on in Jensen and Matiassen's room when we arrived that evening. Tone was asleep in Mama's arms when Mama carried her into the house. Josef and I stood in the front hall like two strangers while Papa went to the shed for firewood. I had a sister, and the sea had been silver-gray when we left Kristiansand. Papa lit Matiassen's lantern and disappeared into the darkness surrounded by the bluish light. After a while he returned with an armful of firewood and the lantern dangling from his forearm. Josef and I watched as he made a pyramid of dry birch kindling and lit it in the black stove from Drammens Ironworks. Soon the fire was blazing brightly; we heard the cheerful rattling of the black iron plate engraved with a couple dancing close together beneath an equally black, shining sun. Josef and I sat in front of the stove while Papa was upstairs looking after Jensen and Matiassen. I heard Papa talking, but neither Matiassen nor Jensen came down to see the baby. It was just the four of us. Papa rolled up his shirtsleeves and wound the Junghans clock. The gleaming clock struck each hour and half hour loudly; it had once had a carved eagle at the top, but Papa had burned the eagle the day the war broke out. Now he adjusted the hands to show the correct time and set the pendulum in motion. He turned on the wrought iron lamp, Tone opened her eyes slightly, and soon the heat from the fire streamed toward my face.

I remembered everything.

It was as though Tone's life rolled slowly like a film in the darkness overhead; everything I thought I'd forgotten, everything I didn't think I had noticed, everything I did in fact remember. Tone's life glided past me like the English bombers high above the clouds.

I wished it were wartime again.

I remembered Tone's baptism, when I sat between Mama and Papa in the front row at church. Jensen sat beside Papa wearing his thick glasses on his nose, and next to him, by the center aisle, sat Josef in his uniform jacket. Suspended in front of us was the pulpit with its painting of the three evangelists by a young man from the parish; I gazed up at the three Roman arches, and at the altar painting of the Ascension with its rolling, ashen landscape and the outline of Our Lord's feet still visible on the ground.

Tjomsland stood inside the altar railing in a long black cassock. I turned my head slightly and saw Papa's face in profile: the high forehead with its irregular furrows and the hair brushed back smoothly. I remembered the candles, how they burned steadily while Tjomsland turned toward the altar and folded his hands to pray. I remembered that it was so quiet I heard the wax dripping onto the floor, and I saw the bright, pure, bluish core in each flame.

As we stood in the churchyard afterward, near the two iron slabs with old-fashioned writing, we cast long shadows across the cemetery. Anna had climbed down the steep steps from the organ loft and stood with Hans and Jon and Tilla. We were surrounded by people from the parish whom Papa had known in another life, and now they all came to greet him. Sløgedal and Tjomsland, and even the sheriff, came and shook hands with Josef and Jensen and Mama. It was the first time Josef and Mama had met the sheriff; Josef beamed instantly, and after shaking hands he stayed beside the sheriff until we were ready to leave. I remembered all of us standing there. The worship service was over; Mama held Tone in her arms, partially hidden under her gray coat, and I leaned my head back and saw the weather vane in the church tower, black and motionless, pointing north. I remembered that Tone cried just before and just after the actual baptism, but when Tjomsland poured water over her head, the crying stopped. There was a moment of complete calm; she lay perfectly quiet, looking up at him in wonder.

I remembered the baptism and I remembered the winter evening three years later when Tone burned herself on the stove in the living room. She was running around naked, the fire was blazing, and no one was there when it happened: she bumped into the glowing-hot stove, right by the words *Drammens Ironworks*. I remembered her screams and how Mama and Papa came running, and I remembered that they later teased her about being branded with *ns* on one buttock.

I lay in the dark and thought about the orange crate that once flew across the China Sea filled with oranges; I remembered the first time Tone slept in it, her face defenseless and turned to the side, her hands barely open in the semidarkness. I remembered the day she was big enough to sleep in the bed with me. How Tone and I lay side by side in the little room, how she lay without moving and listened to me tell about Uncle Josef, who had fallen out of the carriage long ago and hit his head on a rock, about Eugen Olsen at Dikemark, who always thought the building was burning, or about Mama and Papa walking along the road in the dark, years before either Tone or I existed. Her eyes always changed when I told her things: first they grew large, then distant, and sometimes they also grew dark and fearful. At times she woke up at night because she had nightmares about something I'd told her before we went to sleep. I said that Jensen was Satan in disguise, that Matiassen unscrewed his head and put it in a box under his bed every night. That they peeked down at us through the knotholes in the floor. I turned out the light, but later awoke with a start because she was kicking her legs under the duvet and calling for Mama. Tone shouted, and soon we heard footsteps in the hall, the door to our little room opened, and Mama came toward us with Matiassen's miner's lantern in her hand.

Mama sat down on the edge of the bed and Tone crawled into

her lap sniffling. The bomber planes flew past, soon everything was quiet. I heard my voice shouting that she had to crawl forward. The cart had tipped over, time had stopped, but she had heard me. She had crept forward, even though time stood still.

8.

In a way it was easier that Mama wasn't in the house. Josef lay in his room humming to himself, Matiassen sat in the garden even if the weather was chilly, the siblings sang the table grace while Papa was in the barn caring for the cows and the horse.

It was almost a relief.

Every day I knocked on the siblings' door, and I sat at the table and sang with them more and more often.

At first it seemed unnatural.

"Why is he here?" Nils asked.

All eyes turned to Lilly, but she didn't say anything.

"Is he going to eat here?" said Nils.

He sat staring at me with his spoon in his hand. I looked at Lilly.

"He can do that," she replied.

So it was decided. They placed an extra chair between Ingrid and Erling. We sang "Blessed Lord," Lilly looked at me, Nils looked at me, Erling's head wobbled; everyone sang except for Ingrid, who howled, and after that Lilly dished up soup for each of us.

"Please eat," she said.

We ate in silence, and afterward everyone licked their plates clean. I had a tin plate, just like the others. After a while it was almost natural. Every afternoon after school I went upstairs and knocked softly on the door, and the table was set for me. No one asked why I sat there. Papa ate alone down in the kitchen, while I ate with the siblings upstairs. It was almost natural. After we had eaten,

Lilly cleared the table so I could sit there to do my homework while Ingrid and Erling watched.

In the evening Papa came to get me. We heard a soft knock on the door, Lilly opened it, and Papa stood out in the hall.

"What do you want?" Lilly said.

"It's bedtime," said Papa, looking at me. "Are you coming?"

I slid down from the chair and left the room as the eyes of the five siblings followed me. At the doorway I turned around.

"I'll come back tomorrow," I said.

Erling gradually lost interest in my schoolwork. Instead, he sat on his bed gently thumping his head against the wall while he watched Sverre crawl around on the floor. Only Ingrid seemed genuinely curious about what I was doing. She moved her chair closer and watched while I wrote in my notebook. I tried to teach her the alphabet; I drew an A, and then she drew something that looked like an A.

"Say A," I said.

And Ingrid said something that perhaps was A. After that I drew a B; she copied the letter on a piece of paper as well as she could, and we continued like that until Papa came to get me.

"Good night, Ingrid," I said in the doorway.

She didn't say anything, but gave me a gentle look.

One day she was allowed to go to school with me.

She was, after all, nine years old.

Lilly packed a lunch for her, tied a ribbon in her hair, and gave her words of advice and encouragement, and when we finally set off down the road, the other siblings stood by the window watching us. We walked the two kilometers to the Hønemyr schoolhouse slowly. The sky was almost dark when we left, but it grew lighter on the way. I walked ahead, Ingrid a few meters behind. I heard her uneven, slightly halting footsteps, and it was almost as if Tone were walking behind me kicking pinecones and pebbles so they bounced into the ditch. I stopped and pointed to Lake Djupesland in the dusky light.

"Look," I said. "We've been there. Do you remember that?"

Ingrid nodded, and we continued walking. She lost her breath quickly, so we had to stop often. Sometimes she took a bottle of juice from her backpack and stood drinking it by the roadside for a long time as juice ran from the corners of her mouth.

That's how we got to school.

Nils Apesland stood by his desk as usual when we came in; he took Ingrid's hand and asked her name.

"Her name is Ingrid," I replied. "Can she be here during the class?"

"How old are you?" Nils asked.

"She's nine; she can sit at my desk. She doesn't say anything. She's mentally disabled, you see."

Nils stood in front of us, directing, and we all sang while Ingrid sat with her hands folded on the desk, silently observing the other girls. Nils Apesland wrote arithmetic problems neatly on the blackboard and we all had to copy them in our notebooks; Ingrid got a piece of paper on which she tried to draw numbers too. During recess, Ingrid was allowed to erase everything on the blackboard. I showed her how to dip the sponge in the water bucket by the teacher's desk, and how to wring it out before she began, and in the end she finished the job herself. Then we put on our coats. I found a cloth and wiped away the worst dribble from her cheek and jaw, and we went outside where the other children were playing. Ingrid stayed right behind me, followed me like a shadow, out onto the steps and into the front yard. I showed her the shed with two outdoor toilets, and was aware that the others were looking at us.

"What's wrong with her?" somebody shouted.

"She's mentally disabled," I answered.

Everyone was silent. Ingrid looked at me.

"Is she crazy?"

I shook my head.

"She's not crazy, she's disabled," I said.

"Why doesn't she say anything?"

"She doesn't talk."

"She's disgusting."

Again there was silence. Ingrid kept her eyes on me; her mouth was half-open and a little saliva trickled from the corner of her lips. She waited to see how I would respond.

"Who said that?"

No one replied.

"Look, she's dribbling!"

Ingrid regarded me silently, and I didn't know what to say, I just stood there with my hands clenched, as if ready to fight. At that moment Nils came to the door and called us in, the group broke up, and Ingrid and I were left standing alone.

Later, after we went back to our desk in the classroom, Nils put his hand in his pocket and pulled out one of his snakes. Maybe it had been lying there the whole time, maybe it had been curled up in the leather bag on his desk. Everyone was startled. The snake was very dark, and not as large as the ones he had shown us before.

"Look at this," he said. "I've had this with me the whole summer. It's been so good, so good."

Nils held the snake in the air by its tail and began walking along the rows of desks.

"Does anyone want to say hello to it?"

No one replied. The only sound was his footsteps crossing the room.

Nils came toward our desk, stopped there, and carefully put the snake on the desktop in front of Ingrid.

"Look how good it is," he said quietly.

At first the snake lay very still, but then it began gliding slowly toward Ingrid. Everyone turned to stare at the snake as it wriggled forward.

"Ingrid isn't afraid," said Nils calmly. "Look, Ingrid, put out your hand."

He took her hand and laid it flat on the desk. The snake immediately went closer, crawled along her fingertips, its tongue flicking, then lifted its head and continued across her palm and up her forearm.

"Ingrid isn't afraid," said Nils in a gentle, confidential tone. "Ingrid knows the snake is good."

And that was true. Ingrid sat there with her hand outstretched as the snake made its way across her palm. She sat there without howling, while the snake slowly wriggled up her forearm. She wasn't afraid, she seemed to know the snake was good and let it continue up her arm, but she didn't look at it. She looked at me. She just sat looking at me, waiting for what I would say. When the snake came to the sleeve of her dress by her elbow, it turned its head and slithered back down her forearm, and it was heading toward the desktop when Ingrid suddenly put her hand on my arm. The snake stopped at once. It pulled back its head in a flash. I saw the flicking tongue and didn't dare to move. Then the snake slowly wriggled off Ingrid's hand. I closed my eyes, and felt it slither up my arm.

Afterward we walked the two kilometers home. I walked ahead, Ingrid a few meters behind me. Now and then I stopped to wait for her. Although it was late autumn, the sun was shining and the weather was quite warm. Ingrid was tired and thirsty, but her juice bottle was empty. She walked slowly, dragging one leg a little. Her shoes were covered with gray dust. She had looked at me expectantly, or perhaps it was devotedly, and then she had let the snake crawl up my arm. Before long we could see Lake Djupesland, then we passed Jon Båsland's hayloft, and at last we saw the milk platform by the roadside.

"Come on, Ingrid!" I shouted. "We're almost there now!"

I stopped at the crossroads and waited while she trudged the final distance. Then I saw she had wet herself, but I didn't say anything.

That's how we got home.

9.

A strange closeness had developed between us. Something in Ingrid seemed to soften, to open up and turn toward me. It was the same thing that howled in pain at times, and at other times understood everything I said. It had softened and turned toward me. She had wanted to give me the snake, she knew the snake was good, and I'd shut my eyes and let it happen.

We sat next to each other at the table upstairs, and she watched while I wrote. She saw what I did, then drew letters herself, and they became almost an A, almost a B. She did her very best. She gazed at me with her gentle eyes, and did her very best.

One day Ingrid took my hand and led me downstairs and out across the yard. I followed reluctantly.

"Where are we going?" I asked.

We entered the woods, following the path I had taken so many times before. Ingrid tugged and pulled at my arm with a laugh that almost couldn't be called laughter, and soon we saw the lake shimmering beyond the trees. We made our way over outcroppings, dry moss crunching under our feet, and tramped through marshy areas that now had a brown sheen; the bog cotton was white, tousled, and utterly still in the autumn sun. Ingrid walked a few meters, stopped, turned around, waited, went on a few meters, turned around, waited.

She continued like this until we reached the small beach. The lake was dead calm by the shore. Farther out, small ripples glittered in the sunlight. The sandbar was barely visible, and I saw it was flecked with white bird droppings.

"What are we going to do?" I asked.

Ingrid looked at me and howled softly.

"Should we shout?"

She nodded, so I shouted. The sound echoed from the tall pine trees on the other side, but nothing happened, no bird was hidden among the branches. We were completely alone. A faint murmuring could be heard in the pine trees above us, almost like the day we sat there with Tone and Erling, and Mama swam out to the sandbar. I shouted several times, my voice seemed strange and unfamiliar as it was flung back and forth across the water. Ingrid howled, but not loud enough to cause an echo. I have no idea how long we kept on, I only remember that at some point I turned to look at Ingrid and she was taking off her clothes.

"What are you doing?" I asked.

Ingrid sat down in the sand, took off her shoes, and drew her stockings below her knees. She looked up at me, then pulled her stockings off completely and placed them in the sand next to her shoes.

"We can't go swimming now, Ingrid," I said. "The water is ice-cold."

But Ingrid did not stop, for once she didn't pay any attention to what I said. I stood watching her, my dark shadow stretching across the sand and up a slope of bare rock. Although it was late September, the sun was warm on the beach. I felt it on my back and neck. Ants crawled into Ingrid's shoes; a scattering of insects flew across the water, some came too close to the surface and small, indistinct rings spread out from where they lay helplessly on their backs. I sat down in the sand next to Ingrid, kicked off my shoes, and pulled my socks down over my toes. Ingrid stood up, drew her wool dress over her head, and threw it onto the rocks behind us. I took off my trousers and shirt, and when I stood there in only my underwear I felt the chilliness in the air. Ingrid pulled off her white wool undershirt, then leaned over, removed her underpants, and was completely naked. I hesitated for a moment. I looked at Ingrid. And she looked at me. I saw she was not embarrassed, and was not ashamed. She seemed completely free. So I did the same. I stood naked beside her, with an unreal, fluttering feeling in my chest. I felt as if I had slowly broken loose from myself, and I rose above the water, high above the forest. I saw the pale, transparent hairs on the back of her neck, how they shone in the sunlight, and goose bumps ran down my arms. Ingrid waded into the lake, and gave sort of a squeal when the water splashed up around her thighs. I waded out with her, our feet sank in the coarse sand, the water covered our ankles and calves and made them numb. It was icy cold. Much colder than I had imagined. We stood beside each other as the water grew calm around us. Twigs and swollen pinecones floating in the water washed against the beach. I began to feel a tingling in my feet, in my instep, and around my ankles. It was as if a poison were spreading up my calves, knees, thighs. I looked at Ingrid, her tongue glistened and her breasts had goose bumps. Ingrid looked at me, and I was almost not embarrassed; it was good that she saw me, it was good in a forbidden way. We waded a little farther out, the water rippled around her thighs; our legs became strangely short under the water. I didn't think about either Mama or Tone, or about anything else. I shivered and splashed with my hands, water sprayed up around us; sunbeams glistened in the drops and we laughed and laughed, and there was nothing but our laughter to be heard.

10.

Something had softened, something opened in the darkness and turned toward me. I stole up the stairs. In the upstairs hall, I stopped and listened. It was the middle of the night. All the doors were closed; I heard light snoring from Josef's room. Jensen and Matiassen's room was completely quiet. I went to the door of the siblings' room, pushed down the handle. The door was unlocked, but at first I didn't dare to go in. For a long time I stood staring into the room from the doorway. I heard the soft, shifting sounds of five sleeping people.

I cautiously lay down beside her. She was awake, her eyes were shining, but she didn't make a sound. Ingrid lay staring at me; I felt that, even when I closed my eyes. I felt her warmth, I thought about Tone, I thought about the bird on the sandbar, and we lay like that for a long time without a word. I must have fallen asleep, but was awakened by someone walking across the room. Someone stood in the middle of the room looking at me. It took several seconds before I realized who it was. She looked different in the dim light; she was wearing a long nightgown, her hair hung loosely over her shoulders. I don't think she saw that I was awake. I knew she was mentally disabled of course, but when Lilly stood looking at us that night she seemed to understand. I lay with my eyes almost closed, barely seeing her. Maybe she smiled; she radiated gentle love, and maybe I confused her with the angel in the meetinghouse, the one hovering above the man with the hoe. For a long time she just stood there looking at Ingrid and me. Ingrid was sound asleep next to me, I felt her breath on the back of my neck. I closed my eyes. Then Lilly sat down quietly on the edge of the bed. I heard her breathing, and then I felt her stroke my hair. Lilly gently stroked my hair, at first hesitantly, tentatively, but then the uncertainty faded away and she caressed me as if I were her child. In my mind I saw Ingrid howling,

Erling wobbling his head, Sverre crying and soiling his pants, and Nils grinning as he always did. My mind pictured the whole flock of siblings walking toward the house in the glow of Matiassen's lantern that winter evening. Mama went first, Papa was last, and I walked between Ingrid and Erling. Lilly stroked my hair. I don't know how long she sat there, it felt like an eternity. She murmured something to herself. Maybe it was *yes*, maybe it was *no*, maybe it was just *thank you*.

11.

I was awakened by Sverre and Erling, who stood by the bed gaping at us; sunlight streamed into the room somewhere behind them, the dust sparkled, and Sverre laughed when he realized I was awake. I got up quickly, hurried downstairs, and put on my clothes. Papa was sitting at the kitchen table; he looked up, but didn't ask where I had been.

I walked to school alone, my body still remembering the incident with Lilly. I didn't know what it was, but something had happened, and when I came home that afternoon I ate in the kitchen and did my homework in the living room with Papa. I wrote at the table while he added firewood to the stove, where the couple held each other close and danced under the black sun. When Papa squatted down and opened the stove door, the flickering flames brought life to his face.

"Is Mama coming home again?" I asked.

Papa looked up and waited for a moment as the new logs caught fire, then he closed the stove door firmly, stood up, and walked across the room. He stopped by the table and looked down at my notebook.

"What have you written?" he asked.

"Nothing," I said.

I closed the notebook and looked up at him.

"Is she coming home again?"

Papa went over to the window and stood there for a long time. Outside, dusk had begun to fall, the leaves on the ash tree hung black and motionless. I heard mumbling from upstairs; it was Jensen, he had begun to talk with Our Lord again. I heard him ask a question, then everything was silent, and in that silence he received an answer.

"I don't know," said Papa. "I don't know."

12.

We were excused from school to help with the potato harvest. My fingertips grew sore, mold collected in all the scratches and grooves, and my hands looked like an old man's. Now and then Josef came out on the front steps and stood there with his arms crossed, as if he were lord of the manor and had put the rest of us to work. Anna and Hans came to help, and I heard them speaking softly with Papa; I knew it was about Mama, because when I came closer they stopped talking. After we were finished, piles of potato tops lay in the field, and the remainder of the Virginia tobacco plants from the war still stood there with rustling leaves and rust-colored flowers that swayed in the breeze. Papa and Hans put the potatoes into wooden crates, harnessed the horse to the cart, and drove them into the hay barn. The crates were stored there, smelling of mold and dark autumn evenings when the first stars appeared above the ash tree.

I knocked on the door upstairs. Footsteps approached on the other side. Lilly opened the door.

"Where have you been?" she said.

"I'm here now," I told her.

Ingrid came to the doorway. She looked at me, and I hardly dared to meet her eyes.

"Are you coming in?" Lilly asked.

"I was just going to say good night," I replied.

"Good night," said Lilly

"Good night," I said.

She shut the door, and I just stood there; I think Ingrid and Lilly did the same. We stood there, all three of us, on our separate sides of the door.

The next day I knocked again. Lilly was clearly glad to see me. They were ready to eat and made room for my chair between Ingrid and Erling, and everything was almost the same. We sang the table grace, no one said anything while we ate, and afterward Lilly gathered up the empty plates. While she was down in the kitchen, Erling crawled onto his bed and looked out the window. I could tell that he saw something out there. He started to laugh, his head wobbled wildly. We all hurried to the window, and I saw someone walking slowly along the road. It was Papa, wearing his cap with fur flaps. He walked down to the milk platform, where he stayed for a long time. Lilly came back from the kitchen and stood behind us at the window.

"What's he doing down there?" she said.

Before I had a chance to reply, the bus appeared at the bottom of the hill, gliding quietly, a veil of exhaust swirling behind it. We watched as it stopped at the milk platform, where Papa stood. Someone got out; Papa helped her, then went into the bus to get her suitcase, and the two stood there as the bus continued along the road. We all saw it. Mama and Papa stood down by the milk platform for a while before Papa picked up the suitcase and they began walking toward the house. It was Mama. She had come back. I didn't know how long she had been away; it felt like a long time. Mama and Papa came walking across the yard, but something about Mama was different. She seemed tired. They stopped several times, and she leaned heavily against Papa while talking into his shoulder. He put his arm around her, and suddenly she straightened up and looked toward the house, directly at the upstairs window where the siblings and I were standing. She raised her arm and waved. I was afraid she would see me and I moved away from the window, but Erling laughed and waved back, Lilly did the same, and Sverre pounded on the windowpane.

I heard them come in the door, I heard Mama's voice in the front hall, I heard her take off her shoes and hang her coat on a hook. Then I heard Josef get up from his bed and go downstairs, and I followed him to the front hall.

It was Mama standing there. But something about her was different.

She knelt down in front of me; her face was changed, and her eyes were shining after the trip in the autumn air. She smelled of soap and exhaust fumes, and another, unfamiliar scent that was perhaps the sea. She hugged me, and the way she held me was both loving and determined. Then she picked me up, and I dangled in her arms for perhaps eight seconds before she carefully set me down on the floor.

13.

It wasn't until the next day that I understood what was different. I saw it when I came into the kitchen in the morning. Mama stood by the counter slicing bread, Papa sat at the table eating. When I came in she turned toward me, and then I saw it.

It was like taking a deep breath.

And then.

That day a different life began. I spent less and less time upstairs with Erling and Ingrid and the others—my chair still stood by the table, but I ate downstairs with Mama and Papa. In the evenings I lay in bed listening to the new sounds in the house; Mama and Papa talked quietly on the other side of the wall, then Papa got up and went over to the stove, opened the door of the stove, and added new logs to the fire.

I awoke to a new day with sunlight from a dull autumn sky. Standing at my window, I saw the thin overnight layer of hoarfrost that had barely begun to melt on the fields' plowed furrows. A bitterly cold morning. When the sun rose above the treetops the leaves on the ash tree began to fall. They loosened and dropped straight down, and during that short flight they dragged other leaves with them. By the end of the morning, the whole tree was stripped almost bare.

Not a word about where she had been.

Not a word about Tone. Not a word. Not a word.

One evening only a few days after Mama came home, there was a knock at the front door. Papa had just put firewood in the stove, and I saw the strip of light that stretched from the half-open door of the stove straight across the floor.

"Please see who it is," said Mama.

I went into the chilly hallway. Someone was standing on the other side of the window in the front door. I pressed down the door handle and felt the night air on my feet. It was Anna.

"So you're answering the door?" she said.

"Yes," I replied.

Anna's cheeks were rosy and her eyes shone, even though she hadn't walked very far. Some strands of hair at the back of her neck had come loose and hung by her cheeks; it made her look younger, and I thought she might have been crying.

"May I come in?" she said.

Anna had not seen Mama since Mama left. They gave each other a little hug, and she stayed for a long time that evening. Anna must have seen the same thing I did. Or perhaps she already knew. Mama said nothing. I should have been in bed long ago, but both Mama and Papa forgot the time. They sat talking about all sorts of things, but after a while I realized Anna had come for a very specific reason. Namely, a Christmas concert in the church. It would be performed on December 23, and she and young Bjarne Sløgedal, the sexton's son, were responsible for providing the music. Bjarne was an exceptionally gifted musician. During the war he had traveled back and forth to Kristiansand to practice on the cathedral organ. Later he would attend the Conservatory in Oslo, and then cross the Atlantic, like Jensen and Matiassen, to continue his studies at the Juilliard School of Music in New York. But this autumn he was only seventeen years old and had been given the task of performing a Christmas concert in the church with Anna.

After all, it was the first peacetime Christmas.

He and Anna had prepared a preliminary program. Mama sat on the sofa with her hands in her lap, listening calmly, Papa stood warming his hands over the stove, and I sat on the piano bench dangling my feet. Anna took a small piece of paper from her skirt pocket, unfolded it on the table in front of Mama, and stroked it with her hand as if it were a piece of clothing she was trying to smooth out. First she would play a short prelude, she said, followed by Hermann Wenzel's "Christmas Day"; then Alma Kleveland would give a Christmas prologue. Next would be Schumann's "Evening Song," and after that Bjarne Sløgedal would play "Good Christian Men Rejoice."

Anna spoke rapidly, and seemed tense. She glanced over at Mama, but Mama sat just as before.

"Then we'll have the evening's speech," she said. "And after the speech I'll play Lasson's 'Sabbath Clocks'—you know that, of course. Then Bjarne will play a fantasy on the national anthem, and finally Syvert Mæsel will give a short talk."

Syvert Mæsel was the leader of the Mission Society.

Anna paused for a moment. Mama looked at her attentively. The fire crackled in the stove. No one said anything for a while.

"We also wanted to have someone sing."

Mama still sat without saying a word. Papa turned around.

"And we thought about you, of course."

"About me?" Mama exclaimed.

"You've performed in public before, after all," said Anna.

There was a long pause. Then Mama said: "That was in another life."

Anna looked at her, then at the handwritten piece of paper on the table. Papa opened the stove door and added more logs.

"We'd like you to sing Schumann's 'Evening Song,'" Anna continued. "See, here are the words."

She handed another piece of paper to Mama, who took it half-heartedly, read it for a while, and then abruptly put it down. She looked up at Papa and shook her head.

"No," she said. "I can't do this."

When Anna left, I was sent to bed. Mama and Papa sat in the living room for a long time; I heard their voices through the wall. I heard Mama pacing back and forth, I heard Papa stoke the fire, I heard footsteps in the hall and the front door being locked, and finally I fell asleep.

The next day Mama put on her winter coat, mittens, and shawl, and left the house as dusk began to fall. I ran upstairs and watched from Josef's window as she disappeared down the road.

"Why such a rush?" Josef said from his bed. "Is the Roman Empire burning?"

"It's just Mama," I said.

"Is she going to leave again?"

Mama crossed the yard slowly; her coat was unbuttoned, and she seemed heavy, sluggish. She stopped by the hawthorn hedge to wait for Anna, and then they walked down the road together.

"No," I replied. "I think she'll come back."

A few evenings later Ingrid and I were in the cattle barn with Papa while he groomed the horse. He brushed from the mane to the hindquarters, first against the hair, and then he smoothed the coat with long, supple movements until the whole horse shone in the pale light. Ingrid and I walked quietly across the straw dust in the hayloft and filled our arms with hay that still had a strong, spicy summer fragrance. In the semidarkness I saw the horse cart, but I don't know if Ingrid saw it, she walked silently right behind me. She still had this softness within her, and her gentle gaze still turned toward me. When we returned to the cattle barn, I filled a bucket with water and lay a tuft of hay on top so the horse would not drink too quickly. Then Ingrid and I watched Papa. He had his back to us as he took the horse's hoof between his knees and rubbed it with an oily mixture of animal fat and Creolin that made his hands shiny. I imagined his face, which at times could be deeply unhappy, as if sadness had turned it to stone, while at other times it broke into a smile. At that moment I had no idea what his face looked like. I stood there watching him until he was finished. Neither of us had said a word.

"Where's Mama?" I asked suddenly.

He answered without looking up.

"At Anna's house."

Papa hung his barn jacket on a nail, and then Ingrid and I were allowed to turn off the light switches that were fastened firmly to a board by the door. Ingrid turned off the lightbulb in the hayloft and I turned off the two bulbs in the cattle barn, leaving the horse and two cows alone in the dark.

"Is Mama going to sing?" I asked.

"We'll have to wait and see," Papa replied.

As the three of us walked across the yard I heard the clasps on his boots jingling. Darkness. No stars. Light shone from Jensen and Matiassen's window.

"We'll have to wait and see," he repeated.

14.

The nights were cold, and the grass was covered with frost when I walked to school early in the morning. Ingrid watched me leave from the window upstairs. Nils Apesland stood in front of us and directed while everyone sang; above him hung the Atlas Mountains and the Mediterranean Sea with its dark blue color. The snakes must have gone into winter hibernation deep within the scree near his house, because I didn't see them anymore. Later, when everyone was busy writing, he came over to my desk.

"What happened to Ingrid?" he asked.

"She's at home."

"Doesn't she want to come to school?"

"No," I replied.

I noticed that the whole class was listening.

"Why doesn't she want to come to school?" Nils asked.

"Because she's mentally disabled."

"Maybe she'll come with you tomorrow then," said Nils, returning slowly to his desk.

"No," I said, before he could turn around. "She'll never come back."

One morning I woke up and realized something had happened while I was asleep. I threw aside the duvet, stepped onto the cold floor, and went over to the window. Outside I saw large snowflakes drifting down, and by the time I walked to school, the whole world had turned white. It was still snowing that afternoon—the forest was silently being snowed under and the light appeared bluish among the trees.

Josef was standing on the front steps, barefoot, his shoulders turning white, and he shouted that I must come. His voice sounded strange and different, but I soon understood it had nothing to do with me or with us; it was about the snow falling from the sky.

"Look," he said.

"What do you mean?"

"The angels are dancing until their feathers fly," said Josef.

The snow was already deep in the yard, the pine trees at the edge of the woods had grown stout, the treetops shimmered through the driving snow.

We stood in the doorway for a long time, Josef and I, just looking.

The snow continued all night long. I heard Jensen hobbling back and forth upstairs talking with Our Lord, while snow fell and fell, on the house and the yard and the woods, and deep down in my sleep and my dreams, where everything was silent and white.

One evening I was in my bedroom when Mama put on her coat by the mirror in the front hall. I heard her throw a shawl over her shoulders and disappear into the darkness, closing the door carefully behind her. I waited as she went down the steps outside, and then I followed her. I opened the front door very cautiously and slipped outside. It was cold. Pulling my jacket tighter around me, I paused in the yard and listened. I could tell she was ahead of me; I heard her footsteps going down the road, and when she got to Hans and Anna's house I saw her clearly in the light of their outdoor lamp. She knocked on the door. Anna appeared in the light, opened the door, and let her in. I walked along the hawthorn hedge and into their garden. The snow was almost up to my knees. Through the kitchen window I saw Mama take off her coat and hang it over a chair. She turned, looked toward the window, and fixed her hair a little. She was wearing a dress I hadn't seen before. I stood motionless, thinking she had seen me. But she turned and went into the living room. I stole to the other side of the house, where I could look in through the living room windows, and I saw Anna sit down at the piano while Mama paged through a book of music. I barely heard Anna begin to play; my feet were freezing, my hands were freezing. The piano music was muffled and faint, even though I saw how her fingers raced over the keys. At first Mama stood very still with the book of music in her hands, and then, after a while, she began to sing.

I saw her singing, and I saw Anna playing, but I heard almost nothing. Faint wisps of music and song wafted into the darkness, but I didn't go closer; I just stood there until Anna lowered her hands and turned on the piano bench and said something to Mama. I saw Mama laugh, Anna touched her arm. And in her new dress, I saw very clearly that Mama was pregnant. I looked at her stomach, and I seemed to feel her breath on the back of my neck. Then I followed my tracks back to the road and hurried home.

PART THREE

1.

It took me many weeks to empty the house; I had all the time in the world, calmly went through room after room, threw out most things, and left the large, heavy items until the end. November arrived before the entire upstairs was empty. The ash tree had lost all its leaves. I'd gone in and out of the house so many times the front steps crunched with sand. Now and then I paused in the yard to take a deep breath of the autumn air. Above me, the ash tree's sprawling, motionless branches looked like cracks in the sky.

The garbage bags filled with clothes and shoes were in the hayloft; I had folded everything neatly, tied the sacks with twine, and attached a note about what they contained. All Mama's clothes were to be sent to the needy in Russia. Nothing was to be thrown away. Not even the shoes. Other women would continue to walk in them, somewhere else, preferably in Russia. It was what she wanted. It showed a *Christlike spirit of love*.

Darkness fell early at the end of November and I worked long into the night. I got used to being alone in the house, but I was not used to removing things from the walls: pictures that had always hung in the same place, lamps that had always cast the same shadows on the ceiling. The mirror in the front hall where Josef had smoothed his mustache with a shoe brush every Sunday morning.

Finally, all that remained were the kitchen and living room. In addition to what was already in those two rooms, I collected other things I felt were worth saving: the tin plates, Matiassen's lantern, the bag of Tone's clothes.

One evening I went to work on the tasks that remained. I parked my car under the ash tree, turned off the headlights, and looked up at the house as it stood there in the darkness. It was raining slightly; I felt the drops in my hair when I let myself into the house. I turned on the lights in the front hall, the kitchen, and the living room. Then I squatted in front of the stove, laid in pieces of kindling, struck a match, lit a wad of newspaper and birch bark, and waited with the stove door open until I was sure the wood would burn. While the warmth slowly spread in the living room, I made coffee and cleaned out the kitchen cupboards. The hours went by and the kitchen became increasingly empty, until in the end all that remained was the cold echo of my footsteps, the flickering fluorescent light in the ceiling, and the unreal feeling that everything was unchanged, but at the same time unfamiliar.

When the kitchen was done, I took a break, sat down in the easy chair in the living room with the television on, and thought about Josef and Lilly and Ingrid sitting upstairs twenty years earlier watching the *Fleksnes* television series; their laughter and Josef's exclamations could be heard way out in the garden. The past weeks of clearing, sorting, and discarding had brought memories of them closer. I remembered how they gathered in Josef's room every Saturday evening to watch *Krutrøyk*, or the king's New Year speech, or the election broadcasts or political debates with Gerhardsen, Borten, or Bratteli in the studio. They always sat spellbound in front of the screen, Josef on the edge of his chair, Lilly on the edge of the bed with Ingrid, who seemed totally absorbed as she calmly licked around her mouth. They sat there and concentrated on following the program, and none of them said a word until the broadcast was over, the nation's patriarchs stopped talking, and the screen went dark. Then Josef might stand up and say:

"Well, well. So Christmas came again this year."

The resounding strokes of the Junghans clock on the wall echoed in the Steinway piano, and I sat amid the fading sound until it died away. Herbert Andersson's painting of Tone holding the kitten hung between the windows that faced south; in the evening light you could no longer see what she had in her arms. I sat in semidarkness as the walls and ceiling flickered in the constantly shifting light from the television, and was about to get up to light the lamp on the piano and continue working when there was a knock at the front door. I'd been alone in the house so long I hadn't thought about the possibility that someone might visit. I rose quickly, glanced briefly toward the front hall, then went and opened the outer door.

Anna stood on the front steps. It was still raining a little; raindrops glistened in her hair, and I heard water dripping from the ash tree onto the hood of my car.

"So it's you!" I exclaimed.

"I saw the lights," she replied.

My heart was pounding in my chest; I'd stood up too fast. For a moment, everything went black and I held on to the doorjamb.

"I just wanted to see how you are," said Anna.

"Thanks," I said. "I'm fine. I'll be finished soon."

Anna's face had become leaner, moisture ran from one eye, perhaps a drop of water from the ash tree had struck her as she crossed the yard. She was now eighty-six years old. Her skin seemed thinner, almost transparent; her entire being had become somehow transparent.

"Come in," I said. "You can't stand out there in the rain."

"I hadn't planned to come in," she said.

"Well, then things will be different from what you planned," I replied warmly, and opened the door wide.

Only her voice was unchanged—her voice, and the way she moved; when she entered the front hall she walked the way she had for as long as I could remember, her body still nimble and tough. She hung her thin gray summer coat on the banister, wiped the moisture from the corner of her eye, and turned toward me.

"And you?" I said. "How are you?"

"I've gotten old," she replied.

"Do you still play the piano?"

"Not for a long time. My fingers aren't up to that anymore. Neither is my heart."

I nodded and said, "Please come and sit down in the living room for a while. I've made coffee."

"That would be nice," she said. "Now that I've come this far. And if you haven't thrown away all the chairs," she added with a smile, and I realized her smile was the same too.

I turned on the sconces with dangling glass prisms that hung on each side of the wall clock in the living room. I lit the piano lamp and the table lamps on either side of the sofa, so when Anna came in, the room was almost completely light. I managed to clear away the worst of the mess, then went to the kitchen and put on the kettle for a new pot of coffee. Anna had pulled out the piano bench and was sitting at the edge with her hands folded on her knees. She had a thin flowered shawl over her shoulders, and when she sat like that she looked younger than when she was standing. Her hair was disheveled and matted down on one side, and in the bright light of the piano lamp it looked thin and luminous, like a halo. I suddenly felt sorry for her, but only for a moment, because I was moved by the fact that she had come. Anna somehow brought back the old life, everything that had been, and that in some way still existed if we began to talk about it. I switched off the television and turned my easy chair toward the table.

"Sit here instead," I said.

The kettle bubbled and gurgled in the kitchen as I found a package of cookies I'd bought and emptied them onto a plate I hadn't cleared away yet. When I returned to the living room with the coffee and cookies, Anna was sitting in the easy chair, and I sat down on the piano bench.

It was good to have her there.

"You've had a big job here," she said, looking around.

"All that's left now is the living room," I said.

She nodded. The fire burned brightly in the stove.

"I'm looking forward to finishing. It's taken a long time."

She nodded again.

"I know it takes time," she said.

"I don't know what to do with many things. I can't just throw everything away after all."

Anna looked at me.

"Take the time you need," she said.

My eyes wandered to the opening in the stove where you could see right into the fire; I saw the couple who still held each other close and danced under the black sun. We sat for a while talking about one thing and another as the steam rose from our coffee cups. Then, when we didn't seem to have anything else to say, I brought out the bag of Tone's clothing.

"Look what I found. This has been lying here for fifty years."

Anna seemed to stiffen when she realized what it was. She unfolded Tone's pale yellow sweater, laid it across her thin knees, and stroked the material over and over again.

"Where did you find this?" she asked.

It had been many years since I had talked about Tone with someone who had actually known her, someone who remembered how she talked, how she laughed; someone who hadn't just seen Herbert Andersson's painting, but who had actually seen her run around in the garden that now lay in darkness outside the windows. I thought Tone was gone, but she was still here. Even now, after an entire lifetime. She hadn't gotten any older, she clung to the kitten, or the kitten clung to her. Tone grew clearer the more we talked about her.

I heard her voice, I heard words and sentences she spoke, I saw her hands, I saw her clothes draped over a chair, her ribbon thrown on the floor. I saw the sunlight in her hair.

"How old would she have been?" Anna asked.

"Fifty-four," I replied.

She regarded me silently for a long time.

"Are you sure?"

I nodded.

"Yes," I said.

A car approached on the road outside, but it wasn't coming to us, it didn't slow down; it drove farther north in the darkness, and then everything was quiet again. Anna shook her head.

"I can still hear her laugh," she said.

Anna stayed for a couple of hours; the clock had just struck eleven when she stood up to leave. The fire had gone out in the stove. I went into the front hall with her, and felt the cold draft along the floor as I watched her put on her coat. I had thought about saying something, something from me to her, something about how she had brought back the old life, how all of a sudden Tone had come so close. I opened the door and went out onto the front steps with her.

"Thank you so much for coming," I said.

"Of course. It's the least I could do," she replied.

"It was good to see you," I added.

"It was good to see you too," she said.

As I walked across the yard with her I had an unpleasant prickling sensation in one leg, it seemed as if my feet would not carry me. However, it gradually felt better, and after a while I was just fine. I'd had the same feeling as when I carried Mama from the chair in the garden some months earlier; she had been so light, I could have just continued, down the road to the milk platform, and it would have been like carrying almost nothing.

We paused where the road began to curve down the hill and I saw her house, the warm light from her kitchen window.

"Did you know that Hans carried me all the way from the hay barn to your place?"

Anna gave me a questioning look.

"He carried you?"

"He was the one who found Ingrid and me. We had hidden in the grass by the hayloft. He didn't say a word, he just picked me up and carried me the whole way."

Anna stood there as if she had to think carefully how to reply.

"You and Ingrid had been hiding?" she said.

"Yes, we lay in the grass and prayed."

"And then Hans carried you down to our place."

I nodded.

"Yes," I said. "That's what happened."

At that moment I was overwhelmed by a deep, defiant sadness and I had an urge to give her a hug, put my arms around her; I wanted her to say something more, tell me something I didn't know. Something. Something.

Anna turned to me in the dark.

"Are you managing all right?" she asked.

"I'm managing just fine."

"That's good," she said.

Then she turned and walked away. I didn't do anything, I didn't say anything, I just stood there and watched as she walked the short distance to her home.

2.

After she left I immediately began clearing out the desk in the living room. That's when I found the contract, the cover letter, and, later, the photographs in Mama's confirmation Bible. I also found a letter that stood out from the other things. It was written in Papa's sloping, somewhat shaky handwriting on very thin, almost Bible-thin, paper. A duplicate. The letter, dated July 12, 1973, was addressed to the Child Welfare office in Stavanger, which over the years had changed its name to Stavanger Social Services. In it Papa gave notice to terminate the caregiving agreement.

For twenty-eight years he and Mama had been bound by the contract he signed outside on that dark winter evening in 1945. For a generation they had demonstrated a *Christlike spirit of love*, and in the summer of 1973 he sat alone at the kitchen table and summed up their entire life.

A one-month notice was still required.

The three brothers, Nils, Sverre, and Erling, had been released from the contract since the fall of 1963, although they had come back each Christmas and each summer since then. Christian Jensen had died, as had Matiassen. But patients had been at the house the whole time. Jensen for almost twelve years, Matiassen for twenty-two years, the three brothers for eighteen years, Josef for twenty-nine. And then there had been Mina Jensen's five-month intermezzo starting in the fall of 1948, when at long last she was reunited with her son Christian.

Lilly and Ingrid were still there.

Papa sat alone at the kitchen table, he wrote slowly, and tried to include everything. He wrote about the wild dance that had finally worn out Jensen completely; he wrote about Matiassen, who at the end had to be carried back and forth from the stool under the ash tree; about Erling's increasing migraines; about the fight upstairs; about Sverre, who ran out of the house and lost his way in the woods more and more often. He wrote about Josef's singing, about the wandering cup and the medal for courage. He wrote about everything—the way it had been, the way he remembered it.

He did not write anything about Tone.

At the very bottom of the thin sheet of paper was his signature. Mama read the letter and had nothing to add, even if perhaps she wished he would have written something about Tone. She didn't say anything, only nodded. So he folded the page, put it in an envelope, and walked down to the milk platform in the last of the afternoon sun.

Upstairs, something moved behind the curtains.

He walked the short distance to the milk platform, put the letter in the mailbox, and returned home, slowly and alone. About halfway he stopped, his shadow stretched far across the field. He looked toward the house, toward Mama taking down laundry from the clothesline. He had tried to summarize the last thirty years. Everything fit on an A4 sheet of paper, but he hadn't mentioned one word about Tone.

Several weeks later a green station wagon drove up the road from the milk platform. The car stopped in the yard, and out into the sunshine stepped a man in light-colored trousers; his shirt was wrinkled in the back and the sleeves were rolled up. He walked over to the shade of the ash tree to stretch his legs, took off his horn-rimmed glasses, and wiped the sweat from his face with a pocket handkerchief.

The man was Peder Johannessen, department head at Stavanger Social Services. A little later another vehicle arrived and another man got out, district doctor Håberg from Søgne.

It was a warm day, the sun was high in the heavens, and Johannessen had driven nonstop from Stavanger, a demanding four-hour trip. It had taken Håberg forty-five minutes from Søgne. They had come to sign the final papers and thereby end the caregiving contract.

Mama and Papa came out to the front steps, the four of them

stood talking in the shade for a while, and then they went in to the living room, where all the necessary papers were stamped and signed.

Afterward Papa suggested he show the men around the house that had served as a caregiving home for a generation. He showed them the living room and kitchen on the first floor, then the easy stairway to the second floor with its short distance between the steps. They came to the upstairs hall with doors to the right, to the left, and straight ahead. First they went into Josef's room, which was empty now.

"This is where Josef lived," said Papa. "He almost took care of himself. He liked to read. I don't think anyone around here read more books than Josef."

Johannessen took a few cautious steps into the room, the floorboards creaked. He thumped his knuckles against the Jøtul stove, then went over to the window. Papa said:

"And he had an unusually good singing voice."

That was all that was said. Josef's remarkable life briefly and precisely summarized in five sentences. Johannessen and Håberg stood by the window for a while looking at the ash tree, at the tangle of twigs and branches and the interplay of sun and shadow. Then they turned and walked out of the room, and Mama carefully shut the door.

After that the two visitors were shown Matiassen and Christian Jensen's old room.

"This is where Christian Jensen from Mandal and Matiassen from Flekkefjord lived," said Papa. "Matiassen usually sat on a stool out in the garden, whereas Jensen, well, he wrote a whole book of poetry before he came here."

"Really?" Håberg exclaimed. "A book of poetry?"

Papa nodded.

"But his mother burned it."

Again Håberg and Johannessen walked into the room slowly, and again they went to look out the window.

"What did you say his name was?"

"Christian Jensen," Papa replied.

"And the other man?"

"His name was simply Matiassen."

Finally Papa led them to the last door in the upstairs hall. He knocked softly, and they heard a response from inside.

"Who's there?"

"It's just me," Papa replied, leaning toward the door. "There's someone here who wants to say hello to you."

He waited a moment, footsteps were heard inside, and the door opened.

Lilly and Ingrid were still there, and since it was July, the three brothers were at home on summer vacation. The whole flock of siblings was there, almost like the old days.

Lilly lined them up—Sverre farthest away, then Ingrid, then Erling, then Nils, and finally Lilly. When they were children this was a natural arrangement, from the youngest to the oldest. But now it looked a bit disorganized. Sverre had become the tallest. Ingrid was slightly taller than Erling, Nils was a little taller than Ingrid, and Lilly was the shortest of them all.

Johannessen and Håberg crossed the room and shook hands with each one. Lilly made a deep, dignified curtsy as she had done her whole life; Ingrid did the same. Erling just stood there, while Sverre dutifully made a stiff bow.

"So people live here too," said Johannessen.

"Yeah, yeah, by George," replied Nils.

Everyone watched as Johannessen walked around the room. He circled the table with the five chairs. He leaned against the window frame, looked out the windows. He saw the picture of Jesus holding a lamb, and then leaned over to study a framed photograph that hung above Ingrid's bed. It was the picture of her and Tone with the kittens in their arms.

"Who is this?" he asked.

No answer.

"Is it any of you?"

Still no one replied.

Johannessen turned around.

"Are you the one standing there with the kitten?" he said to Lilly, pointing at the photograph.

"No," said Lilly. "It's not me."

At this time Lilly was forty-five years old. Nils forty-three. Erling thirty-nine. Ingrid thirty-seven. Sverre thirty-two. Now they were gathered in the room where the five of them had lived together for eighteen years. Each day they had sung the table grace. In the evening Lilly helped them brush their teeth and saw to it that everyone got to bed, and they lay with their hands folded on top of the duvet while Lilly prayed an evening prayer; then she turned out the light, and they all lay in the dark. They were her children somehow. Even though they got older, they never grew up.

"It was nice to meet you," said Johannessen as he stood in the doorway.

None of the siblings replied, but Lilly curtsied.

They had no idea that the caregiving was now formally ended.

3.

Mama taught Lilly how to dry small bouquets of flowers picked from the garden. The patients at Dikemark had done the same, she told Lilly; the attic above the women's unit had smelled like eternal summer. Lilly picked small bouquets, tied them with twine, and hung them on clotheslines in the attic above Josef's room. Every day she went up to check on them, to see if anything was needed, if everything was as it should be. The flowers hung to dry for several months, but they kept most of their original colors. There were daisies, buttercups, and yarrow in delicate, beautifully made bouquets. At Christmastime Lilly and Ingrid went from house to house in the falling snow and sold them for five *øre* each; the money was to go to missionary work. They stood close to each other on the front steps when the door opened.

"Do you want to buy, ma'am?" Lilly asked.

Ingrid held out the basket of flowers, and people bought the small bouquets. Ingrid received the money in her hand, gave it to Lilly at once, and made such a deep curtsy that snow sprinkled from her shawl and shoulders and her long winter coat spread out on the floor; when they left, there were puddles on the floor where they had stood. They went from door to door until all the bouquets had been sold, and on the way home they stopped at the Brandsvoll store. They were hungry after their peddling, so Lilly bought a package of Gjende shortbread, which they devoured on the spot. Afterward Ingrid was thirsty, so Lilly bought her a bottle of Asina, and one for herself; then of course they needed a snack to keep them going until they reached home, and by the time they left the store there was no longer any money left to send to the missionaries.

After all, it could be called a kind of work.

And so the hours, the days, the years went by. Josef rode home on his bicycle from the public library with his bag full of books; *the Tower of Babel* grew on his nightstand, and he began with the A's once again. Halvard Lange became foreign minister under Gerhardsen,

Jensen held conversations with Our Lord, and Matiassen rocked on his stool under the ash tree.

The starlit sky revolved slowly above the house.

They got meals morning, noon, and evening; they had a bed and a roof over their heads. Matiassen had his stool, Josef had world literature, and Jensen had the magazine from the College of Wooster. They lived isolated from the world, and yet, there were occasions when they entered it.

In May 1949 I was confirmed in our church.

Grandpa came all the way from Oslo, the first time he had seen Mama since the fall of 1945. It was also the first time he saw Astrid.

I wanted the siblings and Josef to be in church.

"I want them all to come," I said.

There was silence for a few seconds. Papa looked at Mama, she looked at me.

"Well," she said. "Why not?"

Lilly washed and dressed the four others upstairs. When they came down Ingrid had a ribbon in her hair, Nils's and Sverre's hair was combed smoothly, and Lilly wore the flowered summer dress with a narrow belt around the waist. I recognized the dress immediately; it was Mama's, but fit Lilly perfectly since they were the same height. Lilly was twenty-one, she was of age, or of age *in theory*. In practice nothing happened, in practice she was the same as always: almost beautiful, almost ordinary—and of age. She arranged the siblings in a row while they waited to leave. Josef came downstairs too, and, as always when he went to church, he was wearing his uniform jacket with the medal for courage on the lapel.

A new pastor had come to the area recently. Absalon Elias Holme, a name worthy of a parish pastor. He stood inside the altar rail in his black cassock and prayed for each of us while the swallows flew back and forth from their nests in the church tower. When it was my turn, Mama and Papa, Josef, and all five siblings rose from the pew. They stood there while Holme laid his hand gently on my head. Nils grinned, Erling's head wobbled, Ingrid just stared, and at that moment I caught the scent of white carnations.

Afterward everyone sat around the big table in the living room at home, and when we had finished eating Josef tapped his knife against his glass, pushed back his chair, and stood up.

"I won't say much," he began. "But what I'm going to say, I've thought about carefully."

Then he was suddenly silent. He stood behind his chair and regarded me with a serious expression while he chewed his mustache and held on to the back of the chair.

"Once when I was a young man I left on a long trip, to the city of Trondheim."

Long pause.

"And in the city of Trondheim I was lucky enough to see the midnight sun."

Another pause. He took a deep breath.

"And in the city of Trondheim I met my young bride."

The room was very quiet, only the soft ticking of the Junghans clock, and the creaking in the ceiling that was Matiassen rocking on his stool above us.

"What I want to say to you on this day is that I've never forgotten the midnight sun, and I've never forgotten my young bride. I want you to know that on a day like this."

Josef and I exchanged glances. It was as though strange words and images drifted like mist before his eyes. Words he almost understood, images he almost recognized. This lasted a few seconds, but then suddenly his face broke into a remarkable smile that made his mustache leap. Still holding on to the back of his chair, he reached for his glass.

"Skoal for the confirmand, and skoal for the missus!" he shouted, and took a drink.

After Josef's short speech, Lilly stood up. The room grew quiet again. Mama glanced at Papa and lowered her glass. Lilly smoothed her dress and stood behind her chair, exactly as Josef had done. The four siblings looked up at her. Perhaps they were surprised; everyone had assumed that only Josef would make a speech, but then Lilly stood up. She cleared her throat, held on to the chair, looked at me, and said:

"I just want to say the food was good."

4.

Months could go by when nothing special happened. The days melted into one another. Morning came, evening came. Breakfast at nine o'clock, dinner at three o'clock, the table grace was sung, Erling's voice changed; during the summer Erling suddenly talked like a man, but he learned to sing in falsetto like Nils. They sang "Blessed Lord." Always "Blessed Lord."

Then suddenly important things could happen.

Like one day in August 1952.

For a long time Mama and Papa had wanted the five to have a visit from their parents. More than seven years had gone by since the evening the siblings were picked up, and nobody knew anything about Hertinius and Rebekka Olsen's life now. Papa wrote to the Child Welfare office in Stavanger to find out how things stood. After a while the office confirmed that Rebekka and Hertinius would like to see their five children again. After that, everything happened very fast. Transportation back and forth was arranged, two assistants from Child Welfare would go along on the trip, and a date was set for the visit. In mid-August the siblings stood waiting under the ash tree, dressed in their very best, when the car from Stavanger drove up the hill. The car stopped, Erling fumbled nervously with the buttons on his shirt, Nils grinned and stuck his hands in his pockets, Lilly made sure that everyone stood in a row. The car door opened and an older man got out; behind him came a little gray-haired woman. They stood and thought for a moment before they approached the group of children.

More than seven years had passed since they last saw them.

Rebekka was the first to say something.

"Is it really you?" she said.

No one replied. Ingrid let out a soft, ominous howl as Rebekka and Hertinius came over and gazed in amazement at their five children. Hertinius lay his large hands on Sverre's shoulders.

"Are you little Sverre?" he said, looking him straight in the eye.

He did the same with Erling and Nils. He put his stonemason hands on their shoulders and asked if they really were his sons. Rebekka clutched a white purse in her hands while she walked back and forth in front of the five children, as if she still could not believe they were hers.

Mama and Papa and the two assistants from Child Welfare stayed in the background the whole time. They had feared some sort of incident might occur, which was the reason for two assistants in addition to the driver. The five of them stood in the shade and watched. Rebekka and Hertinius scrutinized their grown and half-grown children, but nothing happened. No incident occurred. Rebekka opened her purse, took out a tube of lipstick, and gave it to Lilly.

"For when you want to find a man," she said.

Lilly curtsied and took the lipstick.

"Thank you, Mother," she said.

Hertinius came forward, but he didn't have any gifts. He pointed at Matiassen, who was rocking on his stool under the ash tree, like he did every day.

"What's he doing?"

Lilly looked at Rebekka, then at Hertinius.

"He just sits," she said.

Silence for a few seconds.

"He just sits?"

"Yes," Lilly replied.

"Yeah, yeah, by George," Hertinius said finally.

Afterward Rebekka and Hertinius went upstairs to see the children's room. Lilly showed them around the way Papa had shown the siblings around that evening in February seven years earlier.

"We sleep here," she said, pointing to the beds. "We eat here," she added, indicating the table. "We have five chairs and five plates. And this is the window," she said, pointing again. "We can look outside here."

Afterward they said hello to Josef, who, as usual, introduced himself as Mama's uncle and a former tenor in the Hope Chorus; and at the end, at dinnertime, the seven sat and ate calmly by themselves around the table upstairs.

When they sang the table grace, it could be heard all the way out in the garden.

Rebekka and Hertinius stayed for perhaps four hours, and left in peace and contentment. Ingrid was silent, Lilly curtsied, Sverre and Nils stood with their hands in their pockets. Erling turned away. At the end, Papa shook hands with Hertinius.

"It was nice that you came," he said.

"We had to see to the children," replied Hertinius.

Then the unfamiliar car drove away and headed west toward Stavanger.

It was the first visit in more than seven years. It had been a success. No incidents. Mama and Papa had shaken hands with Rebekka and Hertinius, and when the car drove away they breathed a sigh of relief. They had heard the family sing the table grace before dinner, followed by quiet conversation. It was the first visit. And it would be the last.

No one knew what the seven had talked about.

5.

In the summer of 1952 we lost one person in the large caregiving house. But before that, we added one.

A new patient arrived in the fall of 1948. I was at home that day, a dreary, gray day; rain streamed down the windowpanes and everyone was inside. I heard a car stop in the yard, but didn't have time to look outside before it had driven away and the front door opened. An older woman entered the hall, arm in arm with Papa. Water dripped from her clothing as she stood just inside the door, wet and exhausted, as if she had been rescued from the sea.

It was Mina Jensen.

She who had once had such great expectations for her son, she who had recognized his talents before anyone else. She who had sent him to America and thought he would return as a pastor. She had waited in Mandal for letters that never came, and had burned his poems while he was still at the College of Wooster, on the other side of the Atlantic.

Now she stood in our front hall, soaking wet.

I didn't know that she existed, that crazy Christian Jensen upstairs actually had a mother. It had never occurred to me at the time.

Mina had difficulty walking, her shoes scraped across the floor, and Papa had to support her the few meters over to the chair Mama had set out. I don't know how it happened, but Mina Jensen had come to live with us. No contract is to be found. But she was to be a patient, just like her son. Perhaps Papa and Mama would get eighty *kroner* a month, perhaps more; she wasn't a child after all.

Mina Jensen sank heavily onto the chair, and all her belongings were in a small net bag she set down beside her. Someone said later that she had stomach cancer. That she would die soon, that this was why she had come. Perhaps this was true. But she didn't look sick, just frail, worn-out, and bewildered, as if she had walked in the rain all the way from Mandal.

As she sat there on the chair catching her breath, a door opened upstairs. I heard unsteady, hobbling footsteps and knew who was coming. We all heard who was coming, everyone except for Mina Jensen. Christian came tottering down the stairs, concentrating intently on holding on to the railing, moving his feet, keeping his arms still. He was thirty-four years old, with a long beard. Pale and thin, he looked like Wergeland, but Mina recognized him immediately, her son who had once been a poet.

"Oh, dear Jesus," she exclaimed.

She got to her feet as Christian made his way down the stairs. At the bottom he stopped by the newel post, his whole body trembled and shook. He was thirty-four, and Mina must have been more than seventy. Her face was sallow, her eyes clouded, but her black hair had no gray and shone in the glow of the ceiling light. She rose from the chair, but once on her feet she must have felt she couldn't walk the few meters over to the stairs, and Christian must have felt his body would not obey him if he let go of the newel post, so they just stood there and looked at each other.

The two of them lived together upstairs. Matiassen moved in with the siblings from Stavanger for a while, and for the first time I heard Jensen laugh. In the evenings I heard Mina and Christian Jensen laughing so long and so loudly you would think they were going completely out of their minds. It was as if suddenly Jensen had forgotten his earlier life as a student and poet, forgotten the wild dance, the burned poems, the dancing devils, the dirty angels, the conversations with Our Lord. Everything was forgotten. Now he just sat up there with his mother and laughed, long and heartily.

Christmas came, and on Christmas Eve Mina and Christian sat with us around the table while Josef stood by the piano and sang. Christian sat there with a full beard, but without his glasses, and then he looked more like Jesus holding a lamb than like Wergeland on his deathbed. In the warm light he appeared older. He and Mina were like an elderly married couple. Mina had her hands folded on her stomach while Josef sang; her hair was pulled back so tightly it shone in the lamplight. Jensen's face and upper body twitched a little, his arms jerked erratically, but otherwise there was nothing conspicuous about him as he gazed attentively at Josef.

When the rest of us marched around the Christmas tree, Christian and Mina stayed seated. They had no gifts for each other. Now and then she leaned toward him and whispered in his ear, and he would nod and gently pat her thigh.

Throughout the winter evenings they sat upstairs and laughed. The nights were starlit, icy cold; the pine trees in the forest creaked in the frosty air.

Or perhaps I was mistaken. Perhaps it wasn't laughter. I just remember the laughter being there the whole time until Mina Jensen died. Suddenly she died. The laughter stopped, the winter was over, Papa took care of Mina Jensen's body, Christian's glasses were back on his nose. His eyes grew large and round. Spring came with birdsong early in the morning before the sun rose. The snow melted, Matiassen sat on his stool under the ash tree, and one morning Jensen was helped into a waiting automobile and driven to the chapel in Mandal, to his mother's funeral.

6.

He followed her three years later, during the winter Olympics, the same winter I took my high school exams.

In the afternoons I sat with Josef, Nils, Erling, and Sverre and kept track of scores. When Hjallis won the 1,500-meter, Josef stood up and saluted; and when Arnfinn Bergmann flew down onto the landing slope at the Holmenkollen ski jump, Erling sat on the wood box and pulled his sweater over his head while he laughed and laughed.

The laughter and celebrating could be heard outside among the snow-laden pine trees.

In the room across the hall Christian Jensen lay curled up in a fetal position. He lay on his bed with his face turned toward the wall. The wild dance had completely worn him out and forced his body to curl up the way it had once lain in his mother's womb.

Papa knocked on the door to Josef's room and asked me to come with him. He needed help and Mama wasn't there, he explained, and then he sent me downstairs to the kitchen for hot water. When I returned, Jensen lay on the bed almost naked. He lay on his stomach, his clothes in a pile on the floor, and his backside was white as snow. He had soiled his pants. I poured warm water into the wash basin by the bed, and stood by the door as Papa wrung out a cloth and washed Jensen.

"Don't leave yet," said Papa.

I emptied the dirty water outside by the front steps; it melted the snow in a large circle and I could see the ground. When I came upstairs again with clean water, Jensen still lay on his stomach, so I helped Papa turn him over. Papa lifted his upper body while I held his legs, but Jensen was heavy and slippery after being washed, his whole body trembled and jerked, and at one point I was about to lose him. Papa managed to push his legs onto the bed again, and then he lay there on his back, stark-naked, with his eyes closed.

I thought maybe he was ashamed.

He no longer looked like Jesus with a shepherd's staff, he looked more like the pencil drawing of Henrik Wergeland on his deathbed: the sparse beard, the fine, sensitive facial features, the closed eyes. It was a different Wergeland from the dreamy poet astride his little horse, Veslebrunen. This was the Wergeland who had written his last poem and would soon die.

Steam rose from the water while Papa wrung out the cloth and washed Jensen's face. The whole time Papa talked to him calmly, almost lovingly, but Jensen didn't open his eyes. Papa dipped the cloth, wrung it out, and washed his neck. Jensen lay there almost without moving, and for a moment I thought he was sleeping, but he wasn't asleep. Suddenly he opened his eyes and gazed straight at me. Jensen looked at me, his eyes calm and clear, as if he had seen everything in life that was worth seeing.

I lifted each arm so Papa could wash his armpits. His arms were heavy, even though they were almost nothing but skin and bone. Then Papa wrung out the cloth again and washed Jensen's nearly hairless chest. It was as if we were in a cavern filled with warmth and quietness, and a kind of tenderness, for rarely if ever had I seen Papa touch a person with greater care and consideration. There was only quietness and warmth and light, and the sound of trickling water each time the cloth was wrung out, and Papa washed Jensen's stomach, and afterward his groin, and then I looked away.

I went down to get fresh water two more times. After that I brought a large, clean towel and Papa's shaving things—the small brush and the razor that could be folded up. Then I watched Papa lather Jensen's cheeks, chin, and throat, and carefully draw the razor in long swipes across his Adam's apple and almost up to his lower lip.

Next I helped Papa put clothes on Jensen. I held his legs while Papa pulled clean underwear over his calves and thighs. Then we put on a white nightshirt that had to be tied in the back; Papa held Jensen upright in bed while I got his hands and arms into the shirt and tied it behind his neck.

"I'm ready," said Jensen, looking at me.

His eyes were large, immobile. It was the first time I heard him speak to me. For twelve years we had lived under the same roof, and now he suddenly spoke to me.

"Now, now," said Papa. "You're not going to leave, Christian. Just lie down."

Jensen looked at Papa for a moment, then his gaze shifted to me—firm, clear, and determined. He stretched out his hand. It trembled and shook.

"You can take me along," he said. "I'm ready."

It was Papa who cared for him during the final weeks. Christian Jensen had become like a child; he lay with his face to the wall and his knees drawn up almost to his forehead, at the mercy of anyone who took pity on him. Papa fed him, but after a while he would no longer eat. Papa turned him, and changed the bed, but at the end Jensen simply wanted to lie in peace, curled up with his face to the wall, as if in terrible shame.

That was how he lay when he died. Like a fetus.

In death the spasms let go, the wild dance was over at last, his body became relaxed and docile; he could lie normally, his body stretched full-length, and he was free.

Christian Jensen was thirty-seven years old.

Like Wergeland.

The night Jensen died there was a huge snowstorm, and it kept on snowing throughout the day while Papa cared for Jensen's body and placed it in the coffin that had already been ordered and brought by bus from Kristiansand. The snow didn't stop. It continued through the next night and during the following morning. It snowed and snowed, deep in the dreams of everyone as they slept. Jensen's coffin was in the hayloft, and when we awoke the third day the snow was a meter deep in front of the house. The road down to the milk platform was impassable. The hearse, which had come all the way from Mandal, stood down there with white curtains in the windows, and was about to turn around.

That's when Papa found the toboggan in the hay barn.

He dragged it to the yard while Ingrid, Erling, Sverre, and Lilly watched from the upstairs window. Nils and I helped carry Jensen's coffin from the hayloft and, together with Mama, we put it on the toboggan.

"Yeah, yeah, by George," said Nils with satisfaction, putting his hands in his pockets.

Papa straightened his fur cap and brushed snow off his shoulders. He pulled the toboggan over to the top of the hill, seated himself astride the coffin, edged forward the last stretch before the slope went down steeply, gave the toboggan a last push, and slid down the hill in the loose snow.

7.

Christian Jensen was gone; there were no more nightly conversations with Our Lord. The magazine from the College of Wooster continued to come to the Vatneli postmaster, but Papa wrote a letter in English explaining that Christian Jensen had died, and after that we no longer heard anything from America. It was the summer of 1952. We had lost one person in the house, and soon I left too. I went to Kvås to attend folk high school for one year.

Papa drove me in the new car he'd bought that summer, a Nash Ambassador, or simply the Ambassador, as Josef called it. When we were ready to leave, everyone stood in the yard: Josef, Ingrid, Erling, Sverre, Nils, and Lilly. Matiassen was rocking on his stool as usual and took no notice of my leaving. Papa started the car, Lilly drew her sweater tighter around her.

"I'm on my way," I shouted out the window.

Josef waved his arm as if he were standing on the deck of a ship sailing for America, Ingrid stared at the car in disbelief, Nils hitched up his trousers, Erling laughed, and Sverre merely stood there.

"Take care, Ingrid!" I shouted.

"Greet the king!" Josef cried.

And with a jolt the Ambassador drove off.

It was the first time I left them. I was sixteen years old. I wore my confirmation suit, had my hair slicked back, and saw the shadow of the car glide along the hawthorn hedge. When I turned in my seat I saw them all still standing in the yard. They looked almost like an ordinary family, and that was the last thing I thought before the house disappeared behind us. They were almost an ordinary family.

While studying in Kvås I wrote letters home, to Josef, to Erling and Ingrid. I never received an answer, but I knew that the letters reached them, and that they were read. Papa told me later what happened: when a new letter arrived, Josef immediately called everyone into his room. It was irrelevant whether the letter was addressed to him or to Ingrid, or to Mama and Papa. In every case, Josef assumed the role of reader and intermediary of the latest news from the outside world. My letters always began: *Dear everyone at home*. I wrote to everyone, but after a while I knew that Josef always read aloud to the others, so I heard Josef's voice as I wrote.

The winter I was in Kvås, Ingrid and Erling were sent to Kristiansand to be sterilized at the hospital on Tordenskjoldsgata, just like Nils and Lilly seven years earlier. They traveled the forty kilometers to the coast, and the forty kilometers home again. I heard nothing more about it, so assumed it happened without protest. They came back after a few days, looking the same as when they left. A few years later, Sverre was sterilized too. And with that, it was certain there would never be any descendants from Rebekka and Hertinius Olsen's large flock of children.

8.

The years went by. Nils came of age. Erling came of age. Of age in theory, yet still children. The wind swept the leaves off the trees, sending golden ripples into the air. The rag rugs froze to the floor. White anemones trembled in the spring. Perhaps they heard the distant hurrahs from the Constitution Day parade at Brandsvoll. Perhaps they heard the old church bell chime in the west. The bird perched motionless on the sandbar. Snow fell in the darkness outside as Lilly prayed the evening prayer. In the meetinghouse, the angel hovered behind the podium with outstretched arms, as if holding a child.

Time flowed through the house.

Now and then, important things happened.

In the fall of 1954 Papa had a visit from an old acquaintance, a man named Oldervik, the parish pastor in Birkenes. They had known each other as students at Diakonhjemmet hospital in Oslo. Afterward, Oldervik had continued his studies at the Norwegian School of Theology and become a pastor; many years later Papa invited him to our parish to give the Sunday sermon. Oldervik arrived on a Saturday in October and stayed with us overnight. He slept in the small bedroom, in the bed where Tone and I had slept. Standing outside with Papa, Oldervik saw Matiassen, who sat warmly dressed in the October sun under the ash tree. Then Papa gave Oldervik a tour of the house, as he always did with new guests. Oldervik met Josef, who showed him his room, the books, and the smiling photograph on his Border Resident card. Finally, they went to see the five siblings, who were sitting around the table.

Lilly had hastily seated the siblings, as if they were about to eat a meal, but they had neither plates nor food on the table. It seemed a bit artificial. They all sat looking at one another with folded hands, then Lilly started singing the table grace, which was "Blessed Lord" of course, and the others joined in: Erling almost silently, Nils and Sverre with children's voices as usual, Ingrid howling softly. A strange silence followed. The table grace had been sung, there was no food on the table, and none appeared to be coming. Papa and Oldervik just stood in the doorway. Everyone waited, but nobody quite knew what they were waiting for.

"This is the parish pastor from Birkenes," said Papa, entering the room.

Lilly glanced at him and her chair scraped the floor as she got to her feet with studied dignity.

"Stand in a row," she commanded.

All five shook hands with Pastor Oldervik from the distant town of Birkenes. Erling became so enthusiastic he wanted to shake hands with everybody, he shook hands with Papa as if it were the first time they had met; he laughed and his head wobbled and saliva ran from his mouth, and finally he pulled his sweater over his head.

Oldervik was silent the whole time.

The next morning Papa and Josef went to church with Oldervik; they sat next to each other on the hard pew and listened to the sermon. That was when the odd thing happened. Well into his sermon,

Oldervik suddenly stopped speaking. He raised his eyes and gazed out at the congregation. There wasn't a sound. All eyes were focused on the unfamiliar pastor standing in the barrel-shaped pulpit surrounded by the three evangelists, and it was clear to everyone that he had lost his train of thought. He began paging hastily back and forth in the Bible, flies buzzed in the window above God's eye, the imprint of Jesus's foot was still faintly visible on the ashen ground. Finally, Oldervik took off his glasses, laid the Bible aside, and began to tell what he had seen at Mama and Papa's home the previous day. He told about Matiassen, who sat rocking under the ash tree and apparently did nothing but chew his saliva; he told about Nils, and about Erling, who had oatmeal all over his face before they left that morning. He told about Ingrid, who could not speak and just howled softly, almost like a song, but without a melody. Everything had made a strong impression. Everything. Not just poor Matiassen. But also the whole flock of mentally disabled siblings. Two sisters, three brothers, all mentally disabled. It was almost unbelievable. Oldervik stood there in the pulpit and confessed that he'd had difficulty sleeping the night before. He had lain awake thinking about these poor people, who perhaps could not be called people, who perhaps reminded one most of animals. It had shaken him. Perhaps they were in fact more animal than human. He had prayed to Our Lord and read his Bible, but nonetheless he was still shaken.

Who could know if they thought like humans?

He did not say anything about Josef, who was, after all, sitting in a pew with a hymnbook in his lap and the Border Resident card in his jacket pocket and following everything attentively.

The incident made Papa furious.

After Oldervik left Sunday evening, Papa had to take a long walk alone. While he was away it started to rain, and he came back soaking wet.

This was the third time they had been compared to animals. The first time was in the report when Child Welfare in Stavanger took the children away; the second time was by the bus driver at the milk platform; the third time was from the church pulpit, by the parish pastor from Birkenes himself.

The sight of Matiassen and the siblings and simple-minded Josef had raised fundamental questions about what it means to be human. Perhaps a natural reaction. Perhaps a natural question. Oldervik had caught a glimpse of them; he had caught a glimpse of himself as well. And he hadn't been sure what he saw. Papa had needed to take a long walk in the rain. When he came back he didn't say a word, but he was more forgiving, and went upstairs to take care of Matiassen.

After that he often spoke about the Oldervik incident. Still indignant, yet lenient, as if the whole thing had been a misunderstanding. Of course they were human. They were happy children. God wanted them to be happy children.

9.

Of course they were human, Matiassen too. Nobody knew how long he'd sat out there on his stool under the ash tree. If one added up all the hours, it must have been months, maybe years. Every day he came out carrying his stool. He walked the few meters over to the tree, and it might take him several minutes of trial and error before he got the stool placed exactly as it had stood the day before, and the day before that. It was a life's work in itself: to sit there chewing his saliva, in exactly the same spot, every day, spring, summer, and fall, when the weather allowed, for more than twenty years. No one took his spot, and no one knew what he had seen. The shimmering light from imprisoned souls. Or only clouds and sky, wind and nothing.

We were all sure Matiassen couldn't speak, but one evening when I was home for a visit—it must have been near the end of the fifties—I heard an unfamiliar voice upstairs.

Herga perga, haura baura.

Papa put his index finger to his lips.

"Listen," he whispered.

I glanced at Mama.

"Who is that?"

We sat quietly looking at one another as we listened to the muttering voice above us, and after a while I realized who was speaking. Matiassen was pacing around his room, where he now lived alone, repeating the same jingle over and over again. Slowly, calmly, monotonously, as if trying to lull himself to sleep.

Herga perga, haura baura.

"He's started to talk," Mama said softly. "Matiassen has started to talk."

The three of us listened and exchanged glances, as if the strange words up there were really meant for us.

Herga perga, haura baura.

Herga perga, haura baura.

"I hope he doesn't bump into the stove," whispered Papa.

We waited silently as we heard Matiassen move closer and closer to the wood-burning stove next to the door, and I realized that Mama and Papa had heard the same thing many times before, because suddenly there was a shriek from upstairs; the voice instantly became loud and shrill and the jingle went twice as fast.

Hekka pekka hekka pekka hekka pekka!

Matiassen had crossed the Atlantic twice, he had seen two continents, and he had also seen how human souls could shine if a person was trapped long enough in total darkness. Once I asked him if he had been to America, once I asked why he didn't have shoelaces, and, one time only, I touched him. Later I showed Ingrid and Erling how Matiassen drooled saliva if he was teased enough and felt he had to open his mouth. I simply waved a piece of straw in front of his face; he held out for a long time, but finally he opened his mouth and the saliva trickled out, yet he never said a word. Not until near the end of his life, and then as a message possibly meant for us. Matiassen always just sat there rocking calmly, the way the ash tree branches swayed above him in the breeze. For perhaps fifteen years he had not said a word, but then—after Jensen died and he was alone in the room—he began to speak a secret, pleading language.

Only once did he become really angry, in fact furious. The cause was unclear. Matiassen and Papa were alone upstairs. They had some sort of disagreement. Matiassen was suddenly beside himself with rage, the saliva flowed, his eyes flashed. He grabbed his stool, raised it over his head, and came toward Papa, ready to strike. Papa grabbed another stool that happened to be there, raised it over his head, just like Matiassen, and they headed toward each other with the stools raised, and neither knew who would strike first. It was very strange. Matiassen, who had been locked in his own blind fury, stiffened the moment he saw what Papa did. He stood there without moving, still holding the stool over his head, but then he lowered it slowly, and stared at Papa in astonishment.

A moment of calmness, a moment of clarity. Suddenly he saw himself, and Papa, and the whole absurd situation. He lowered the stool and carefully set it down on the floor, and Papa did the same. They stood looking at each other, then Papa started to laugh. Matiassen had seen himself. It lasted a few seconds. And perhaps this was the only time.

Matiassen sat under the ash tree less and less. That final summer Papa carried him downstairs in the morning and Matiassen would sit in his spot for a few hours while bees hummed in the treetop overhead. It must have been the summer of 1961. Countless shadows fell gently onto Matiassen's shoulders, his stool creaked in its joints. Then late one afternoon, the stool collapsed under him, leaving Matiassen helpless on his back in the grass. Papa had to use a fireman's carry, which he hadn't done since that summer day sixteen years earlier before the big thunderstorm; he walked to the house with Matiassen dangling over his shoulder, while the stool lay in pieces under the tree. After the sun went down, a woodcock flew across the cloudless sky above the house, and the summer evening echoed with hammering and pounding as Papa put the stool together in the yard and strengthened it with strong nails.

Things slowly went downhill with Matiassen. In the end Mama and Papa were no longer able to have him at home. One winter day an ambulance picked him up and took him to Heslandsheimen hospital, outside Mandal. His stool was left upstairs, stronger and more solid than ever. It must have been thrown away later. I never saw it again.

When spring came, nobody sat rocking under the ash tree. There was only the wind in the grass, the bees in the treetop, the clouds in the sky. At Heslandsheimen, Matiassen had his own room and a new steel chair with a padded seat. On good days he sat rocking in his chair in the middle of his room, and after a while there were deep depressions in the linoleum floor. It was no longer so necessary to place the chair in an exact spot; besides, no one moved it, or took it in because it started to rain. His chair stood there when he slept, and it stood there when he awoke.

The good days gradually became fewer. More and more often he just lay in bed staring at the ceiling, while his jaw went up and down at a furious pace. Papa visited him twice; both times the chair stood in the middle of the floor and Matiassen lay in bed.

Just before Christmas 1962 Mama and Papa drove the Ambassador the forty kilometers to Heslandsheimen in order to visit Matiassen. It was the third visit since he had moved. They brought Christmas cookies and hard candies and caramels from the Brandsvoll store, so he could chew on something besides his saliva.

They inquired at the administration office, and were asked to wait.

Mama and Papa sat down in a small cluster of comfortable chairs, holding the gifts for Matiassen in their laps. Nearby was a Christmas tree decorated with paper chains, tinsel, flags. Heslandsheimen reminded them of Dikemark: the same corridors, the same indefinable smell, doors that locked from the outside. Christmas decorations that would not break.

After a few minutes, a nurse came and told them Matiassen had died.

Papa rose abruptly, letting the gifts fall to the floor.

"He's dead? He can't be dead!"

It had happened in the spring. The room had been cleared out. It had been scrubbed, aired. His chair stood in the corridor. The marks on the floor were impossible to remove. When Mama and Papa arrived, Matiassen had been dead for more than half a year, but no one had notified them. The staff at Heslandsheimen had been told that Matiassen had no children or family, which was true as far as that went.

They stood for a few minutes to collect their thoughts that December day in 1962. They let the news sink in. Then they got ready to leave. Papa slapped his cap against his thigh, he helped Mama put on her coat, and before they left they put the bag of Christmas gifts for Matiassen under the tree, and said:

"Please give this to someone. It's for someone. For someone from us."

Then they left.

It was snowing heavily in the parking area outside Heslands-heimen. The shoulders of Papa's coat turned white, Mama shook the snow from her shawl. They looked up toward Matiassen's room, where another man was now living. Then they got into the Ambassador, Papa started the engine, and they drove home in the falling snow.

Matiassen was gone. No one knew how long he had sat under the ash tree, no one knew what he'd actually seen, but when he stood in front of Papa with the stool raised over his head, he saw himself.

I've decided to believe that's how it was.

PART FOUR

1.

The three photographs were tucked into Mama's confirmation Bible. They had been taken in Oslo in the fall of 1945. In one she is standing by the equestrian statue in front of the Royal Palace, in the second she is in front of the Parliament building with the Freia clock in the background, and in the third she is standing beside the bronze lion outside the Kunstnernes Hus art gallery next to the Palace Park. Grandpa must have taken the pictures. He must have put them in an envelope and sent them to the Vatneli postmaster after Mama had gone home. She must have chosen to keep them. At that time she was thirty-six years old, and had lost her youngest child just a few months earlier. She stands in her gray winter coat with the belt hanging loosely; her stomach has gotten so big she can't button her coat properly. Her hand rests lightly on the lion's mane. She is pregnant. She's not smiling, but neither does she seem sad or dejected. She stands with her hand on the lion's mane while the bronze animal clings to what is actually a flagpole, ready to tear to pieces anyone who might come close.

If anything, she seems afraid.

On the first blank pages of the confirmation Bible she has written a few facts about Tone. About her birth, the blackout curtains, the clouds coming in from the sea, the soldiers singing, the sounds of the city, the rain at night. She has also noted a few things about Tone's baptism, about Knud Tjomsland, who preached on the Gospel of Mark, chapter 10, verses 2–9. *What God has joined together, let not man put asunder.*

At that point, the writing stops.

Perhaps she had planned to continue as Tone got older. At any rate, the final note is about the baptism. Nothing about Astrid. Maybe she didn't dare.

I found the pictures the evening after Anna's visit. As I emptied the last drawers in the writing desk, there lay Mama's confirmation Bible. I opened it and the photographs fell out. In one, Mama stood with her hand on the lion's mane; in another, she stood with the Freia clock in the background. The picture was taken shortly before two o'clock in the afternoon one fall day in 1945. I happened to remember something Mama once said in passing: *I've always felt like an old person.* Maybe that was true. From the time she was thirty-six she was an old person.

Instead of continuing to work that evening I put on a jacket and went out onto the front steps. It was chilly, but not yet completely dark; light still lingered in the western sky. I saw the pine trees behind the house, the contours of the treetops toward the east.

I walked through the damp evening grass and paused not far from the house. All the windows were dark, except for the living room and upstairs in Josef's room, where I'd forgotten to turn off the ceiling light. I saw the filmy white curtains dancing slightly in the heat of the electric radiator. Otherwise nothing. Then I strolled around the house and stood on the hill gazing across the field and down to Anna's house. There was a faint glow from the small lamps in her living room, and the white light of a fluorescent bulb shone above her kitchen counter. I saw the fruit trees in their garden, where a wooden ladder leaned up into one of the trees. Hans must have set the ladder there two years ago in the fall, I thought. He had taken it off the two hooks behind the shed and set it there before he slowly climbed up. It must have been one of the last things he did. The apples were left hanging. The snow came. The ladder stood there. Anna hadn't managed to move it, so it just stayed there.

A faint white mist hung in the garden, as if someone had tried to erase a small part of the world. For a moment I wanted to knock on Anna's door and tell her about the photographs; maybe she hadn't gone to bed yet, maybe she was sitting in the living room reading. After all, she too had been a reader all her life. I started walking slowly down the road, hearing only the sound of my footsteps. Then I paused. A bird appeared to fly right out of the dark treetops. It crossed the sky just above me, chattering strangely, ominously. Suddenly I saw Anna come into the kitchen; she put something on the counter and turned toward the window, but she could not have seen me, because she calmly returned to the living room. I changed my mind, walked back to our yard, and stood for a moment peering up at Jensen and Matiassen's windows before heading into the woods.

The path was misty and unclear, and I kept thinking I should turn back. My trouser legs got wet, but I didn't turn back, I walked on until I saw Lake Djupesland lying ahead of me, dark and still. I didn't find the path Josef used to follow; instead, I made my way through waist-high juniper thickets, which pricked me through my trousers. I crossed a marshy hollow that gurgled underfoot, and followed dim, gray outcroppings to which large patches of soft haircap moss and an occasional pine tree clung. At last I came to the headland and sandy beach where I'd stood so many times before. But never in the dark.

Never in the dark.

I gazed out at the lake. The milky sky gave more light by the water than in the woods, but even so, the sandbar wasn't visible. The water was completely dark and still. I could sense it only in front of me, I could sense how the ground where I stood curved downward. Somewhere it disappeared under the water and continued down into the depths.

I told myself: You should shout now. But I didn't shout.

2.

Almost forty years would go by before I learned what happened when Mama left.

It was the end of July 1984. I was going to visit Papa at the rest home in Nodeland. I turned left by the butcher shop and parked in the shadow of some tall pine trees. Papa had grown weaker, his health had rapidly declined. He became sick in February, during the spring he got thinner and thinner, in April he received the news, in May all hope was gone, and when summer came he got a room in the rest home with a view of the railroad tracks. When I entered his room, Mama was sitting in a chair by the window with a magazine in her lap. I had a feeling that they hadn't talked together for a long time, that they both knew the other knew, and no words were needed.

They waited for the bird to take flight.

An extra bed had been brought into the room, but I don't know if Mama had slept in it. Usually she stayed awake all night. She went to the kitchen herself and brought his food on a tray, she emptied his bedpan, she helped him shave, she helped him into the bathroom and left the door slightly ajar while she waited outside. She had done this before, after all; she knew how to do it, she had been a hospital nurse. She wasn't the one who gave him shots of morphine, but she moistened his lips with a sponge if he tried to talk.

There was a strange, almost lighthearted atmosphere in the room when I arrived.

"Is he sleeping?" I whispered.

Mama nodded.

"Come in," she said.

I sat with her all evening. From time to time a train roared past outside the window and the sound was so deafening I thought the room would split apart. Papa was restless, perhaps the noise of the train penetrated his morphine sleep and awakened him. He received another shot, which quieted him; he seemed to sink into himself, and his lips slid away from each other.

At nine o'clock the evening train from Oslo arrived.

It thundered past, just a few meters away from us. I was sure Papa would wake up again, but he didn't. He lay peacefully, his mouth was half-open, his chest rose and fell. Then everything grew quiet again, and that was when Mama began telling me.

While Papa slept, she told about the fall day when we all walked down to the milk platform with her. She had been wearing her gray fall coat belted at the waist and Papa had carried her suitcase, the same one she used that time at St. Josef's hospital.

She had cared for Tone's body when it lay in the coffin; she had sent everyone out of the room and asked to be alone. She would never have thought she could do that. But she had done it. Dipped a cloth in water and wrung it out, washed the sand from Tone's face. Put the new dress on her, fixed her hair, tied the red ribbon, folded the small hands. And when she was finished, she had gone out onto the front steps, out into the sunshine. She had walked over to the ash tree and seen the place where the cart tipped over. She had seen the dark, wet sand that was still scattered on the grass, and she had said to herself:

I can't be here any longer.

It had been absolutely clear to her, and that made her calm. She had felt a sense of peace, and all at once everything became easier to bear. She had managed to care for Tone's body, and suddenly she knew that she was going to leave. She knew it when she sat with us in church and Josef sang louder than everyone else. She knew it in the days and weeks that followed. She had gone around in kind of a fog, and the only thing she knew was that she was going to get away from everything. She knew it when the bus appeared behind Jon

Båsland's hayloft, she knew it when she knelt down and hugged me and said I must take good care of Josef and the siblings. She knew it when Papa went onto the bus with her. He had put the suitcase on the luggage rack, and she had told herself she would get rid of that suitcase as soon as she got to Oslo. She would get rid of everything. And she would begin with the suitcase. Papa had stood there in the aisle, and when he turned toward her, he was completely changed. Gone was the man who almost never raised his voice. Gone was the man who sat shoulder to shoulder with Josef in church and listened to the sermon each Sunday. Gone were the eleven happy years. It was as if all barriers had crumbled, as if the dam he'd built after the day he came running with Tone in his arms had burst in front of her, in the midst of the villagers and friends in the crowded bus. She had seen directly into a naked, unfamiliar person who wanted something from her that she could not give. She had touched his arm.

"You need to go now," she had said.

3.

She traveled alone the forty kilometers to Kristiansand. It was a warm, sunny afternoon and already nearly a dozen people stood on the platform waiting for the train from Stavanger. She loosened the shawl around her neck, walked to the edge of the platform, and stared down at the tracks. The train was expected a little past three, and she heard the whistle as it approached. The power cables trembled, people around her grabbed their suitcases and coats and pressed closer to the tracks, and as the locomotive came into view the platform shook slightly beneath her feet.

She traveled more than eight hours, through scattered pine forests, across marshy areas that had already turned golden after the long summer. Endless forests flowed by. Small lakes and islands. Now and then a farm, a cluster of farms, a man with a horse pulling a plow, a black line of overturned soil.

She could not get rid of the image of Papa. It was Papa walking there holding the reins, it was our horse with shaggy hair over its eyes pulling the plow and leaving a line of overturned earth behind it. She thought about Papa's eleven happy years at Dikemark, about the road from the venerable asylum buildings to the employee residences; she thought about the frozen snowbanks by the road, and about how she had suddenly stopped and Papa had walked on alone.

She had only touched his arm.

The train arrived at midnight. She had boarded the train in the Kristiansand railway station in quiet sunlight. Now she got off in the crowded Vestbanen train station in Oslo, and it was like another world. Swarms of people surrounded her, even though it was late at night, and she realized this was because the night train to Bergen stood ready to depart on the other track. She was back in Oslo, five years after leaving. She wrapped her coat tighter around her and tied her shawl firmly across her chest. Then she picked up her suitcase in her right hand, walked through the crowd, and found the taxi stand next to the station.

This is what Mama told me that evening at the rest home. She sat calmly in the chair with a magazine open in her lap while Papa slept in the bed next to her. Outside, the sky had become completely dark. I remember my amazement; it was still July, but a deep November darkness lay outside the window. Just Mama's monotonous voice, the November darkness outside, and Papa lying asleep. Or maybe he wasn't asleep. Maybe he just lay quietly and listened.

She told me everything.

She told about the night nearly forty years ago when she arrived in Oslo and sat in a taxi that took her through the quiet streets. She told about seeing her father again in the custodian apartment. How

he helped her with her suitcase. She sat with Grandpa in the basement of the Foreign Ministry housing complex, and somehow it
was like coming home. She told him everything, and his eyes never
left her. She knew he understood. She had come home to the old life,
the life that had abruptly ended the day Grandma died and Mama
gave up her dream of singing. But now, while she and Grandpa listened to the festivity of a Foreign Ministry reception on the floor
above, it was as though she had come back and was going to start
over again. She would start over again, and would begin by cutting
her hair; after that, she would get rid of her suitcase. And then perhaps she could start to sing again. The only thing missing was the
Steinway piano, which she thought impossible to move, and which
now was more than four hundred kilometers away, in a house that
lay forty kilometers from the coast, at the end of the world.

Perhaps she could sing again.

At one point I had to go out and get some air. When I got up from
my chair Mama gave me an accusatory look, but I didn't know
why. I put on my jacket and quietly went out into the corridor. It
was the middle of the night, so I checked with the night watchman to make sure the doors would not be locked when I returned.
I zipped my jacket up to my chin and walked out to the highway
through the November darkness that I didn't know existed in the
summer. Behind me, water splashed in the fountain; ahead of me
was the butcher shop, its red-lettered sign hanging toward the road.
Walking made me feel calmer. I still heard Mama's voice, but it
became increasingly faint. I turned right and continued toward
the train station. No people. No cars. The orange sign at the Shell
gas station glowed, but everything was closed, locked and bolted.
I reached the train station and walked to the platform. Standing
there, I saw a pulsing red light at the far end of the tracks. I didn't
know what it meant—if a train was coming soon, or if the train was

not allowed to continue toward Kristiansand. It wasn't long before I got an answer. I heard long, drawn-out whistles and a faint whoosh from farther up the valley. The sound grew to an avalanche that came hurtling through the night. I stood very still and waited. The train appeared, and the engineer must have seen me, because the locomotive gave a series of short, sharp blasts before rumbling into the station. It was the night train from Stavanger. The cars clattered past me dangerously close; the noise made me shut my eyes, and for a moment it was like being underwater.

Afterward I walked back the same way.

Everything was as before, but I no longer had Mama's voice in my ears, just the sound of water splashing in the fountain. I knocked softly on the window at the entrance, and the night watchman came to let me in.

Things had changed a little during the half hour I'd been away. Papa was awake. Mama had tried to prop him up with an extra pillow behind his back. She was holding a sponge to wet his lips, and it was clear that she had already moistened them several times. He tried to talk. Mama leaned down close to his face as I stood by the door. I saw him say a few words, I heard his voice, I heard what he said; I'm quite sure he said her name. And as I stood there I suddenly remembered the evening we came home from St. Josef's hospital. Mama held Tone in her arms as Papa squatted by the open door of the stove and the flames made his face come alive. And I thought, as I often had, that the two of them were the black, dancing couple that had been cast in iron at Drammens Ironworks. It was Mama and Papa. I'd always known that. Tone had been branded on one buttock, but it was Mama and Papa who danced under the black sun.

4.

At the beginning of March 1946, Mama took the bus alone to Kristiansand. We walked down to the milk platform with her like the last time, but now it was only Josef, Papa, and I. Once again she had packed her suitcase, once again she would be away for a long time, and once again she left for St. Josef's hospital, not far from the Aladdin cinema.

She had the same suitcase as last time.

The bus appeared, it slowed down, and Mama wrapped her coat around her large stomach as much as possible. She waved from the steps of the bus, Josef straightened up and saluted, Papa stood with his hands loosely at his sides. Mama hesitated. Then she came down the steps again, moving heavily; she walked over to Papa and touched his arm, his cheek, and finally went into the bus. The door closed behind her, and Mama was on her way forty kilometers toward the coast.

The date was March 7. The sun was shining, our shadows stretched across the road. I had never seen her touch him that way. And I never saw it again.

She went to the hospital on Kongensgata for the second time. It was the same redbrick building, the same ancient elm trees in the hospital garden, the same sounds from the city as she lay in bed alone. A quiet evening. Freezing temperatures. Elm trees without leaves.

Once again she gave birth to a girl, but this time there were no blackout curtains.

The sky was white. Snow began falling while she slept.

They brought the baby to her in the morning, and she saw the blood pulsing on top of the little one's head. The wind blew from the sea. She thought she heard the German soldiers singing as they passed under her window. The Sisters of Josef cared for her. When evening came, they gently picked up the child and took it to the nursery with the other newborns. She heard the soldiers singing far away, but then she remembered the war was over. During the night she was awakened by babies crying. She lay there listening. None of them were hers. She was sure. None of them were hers.

When Mama came home with the little girl, Josef went to the piano in the living room, struck a key, and began to sing at the opposite end of the scale. I think it never occurred to him that Mama could sing too, not even after the concert at church. For him, she was just *the missus*, the little niece in whose home he happened to live. It was Josef who was the real singer as he stood with his faithful public before him and all the lights turned off, except for the lamp on the piano.

They named the little girl Astrid.

She was baptized in mid-April, but Mama didn't write anything in the confirmation Bible. No hymns, no Bible verses. Nothing.

Maybe she didn't dare.

Knud Tjomsland baptized Astrid, just as he had baptized Tone almost six years earlier. It was a quiet Sunday, heavy rain poured down onto the snow-covered churchyard, and the gravestones were visible now, dark and glistening. Astrid cried during the entire baptism. Tone had gazed up calmly while Tjomsland ran water over her head, but Astrid screamed. We sat there as before, in the front row. I glanced at Mama, while Josef sat beside me in the pew below the pulpit and covered his ears.

5.

For the first few weeks, Mama kept Astrid next to her bed, but this time Papa had made a proper crib with bars and a feather mattress and carvings of summer birds and field flowers on the headboard.

I don't know what happened to the orange crate.

It was still cold early in the day, but by later in the morning the sun felt warm on my face. The siblings sang upstairs, Josef rode unsteadily to the Brandsvoll library. As soon as the snow disappeared Matiassen ventured out into the spring sunshine with his stool. He hesitated for a long time on the bottom front step before finally hobbling onto the ground. Then he took the ten or twelve steps over to the ash tree and he stood there for several minutes before placing his stool exactly where he thought it had been the last time he sat there, several months ago. Little by little, spring arrived. White anemones bloomed in semicircles in the woods. Mama opened the kitchen windows, and she spread our rag rugs on the brown grass so they would smell of sun and wind when they lay on the floor in the evening. I sat on a windowsill with one leg outside and watched everything she did. On the outside wall of the house, flies moved slowly in the early spring sunshine; they were quiet and peaceful, and I tried to catch them in my hands. The next morning they lay frozen to death on the crusted snow. Astrid woke up and started crying, and Mama put down everything in her hands and ran to the crib to pick her up.

One morning Mama stood in the sunshine hanging up laundry, which she did every day; but this day was special, because I recognized the clothes. I recognized the yellow sweater, the pink wool dress, and the brown stockings. She had washed everything, and now she shook one piece of clothing after another, sprinkling drops of water. Mama acted as if nothing was the matter, but I kept my eye on her from the windowsill, and when she had gone inside with the laundry tub under her arm, Ingrid and I ventured over to the clothesline. We smelled the sweet scents of earth and soap and clean, newly washed clothes. Water dripped from the arms of the dress. Ingrid stretched out her hand and touched it very lightly. Then we ran and hid.

6.

Only later did I learn why Mama had washed those particular clothes. Through acquaintances in the Bethlehem congregation in Oslo, Papa had met the Swedish painter Herbert Andersson. Mama had written a letter to Andersson explaining that they wanted to have a portrait painted of Tone, and all they had was the photograph of Tone and Ingrid and me, with the kittens in the girls' arms. They had the photograph, and they had her clothes. Mama ironed Tone's dress in the kitchen, then folded the stockings and knitted sweater, and when I realized what she was doing, I didn't dare look at her; I turned around in the doorway and didn't go into the kitchen again until long after she had finished. She wrote asking Herbert Andersson to paint Tone in the enclosed clothing. And she added further details. She wanted Tone to stand alone. The background could be the same, it was fine to show a little of the forest and the sky, but she mustn't look as serious as in the photograph. Not serious, just a gentle, natural expression. Finally, Mama asked Andersson to paint a red bow, a little to the right of the part in Tone's hair. Unfortunately, she could not enclose the ribbon.

That was all.

As for the black kitten in Tone's arms, Andersson could do whatever he wished with it.

Mama folded the clothes neatly and packed them up with the photograph and the letter, and one morning Papa walked down the road behind his thin shadow. He stood by the milk platform and waited until the bus arrived. After checking one last time that the address was correct, he handed the package to the driver.

"This goes all the way to Oslo!" he shouted over the noise of the engine.

The photograph of Tone, Ingrid, Cain and Abel, and me was sent off with the clothes. It was sort of a sibling portrait. Tone and Ingrid were holding the kittens tightly. Andersson had received strict instructions. Everything was there, except for the hair ribbon.

The whole summer went by, autumn came, and I'd almost forgotten Herbert Andersson in Oslo. However, one day in October a large package came to the Vatneli postmaster, and Papa had to go alone to get it. It was dark when he returned, and he left the package on the kitchen table. Papa's name was written on the gray wrapping paper in large, elaborate letters and, without anyone telling me, I knew it was Herbert Andersson's handwriting.

The package was not opened that evening. Mama put it in the bedroom, and there it stayed for a long time. It was as though both she and Papa had to get used to the idea that the painting was finally finished, that at last it was in the house with us. They had to get used to the idea that they would see her again.

Like taking a deep breath.

And then.

One afternoon when I came home from school it was hanging on the wall. Just above the piano. Papa had hammered in a nail while I was gone, and it was as if the painting of Tone had always hung right there. I saw it the moment I entered the living room, and I saw that Tone stood there alone. Herbert Andersson had followed instructions and painted her in the clothes Mama had enclosed with the photograph. The ribbon was in her hair, and he had left out Ingrid and me, but he kept the kitten in her arms. Nils Apesland had lined us up, raised his arm, and shouted that we must not move, even though we were all standing motionless. Now Tone stood alone with the kitten in her arms, and even if I'd wanted to say something, no one said a word about the painting until many years later.

Only then did I learn that Mama had not been satisfied. She had seen the same thing I did. Something wasn't right. A little girl stood there, and perhaps it was Tone, because she was wearing Tone's clothes and was clutching the kitten, but there was something about her mouth and her eyes that wasn't right. Something about her gaze. Mama had seen it. I had seen it, and perhaps Papa did too, but none of us had said it out loud. Papa had hammered a nail into the wall and the painting hung there without anyone saying anything. But everyone saw it.

The girl in the painting was Ingrid.

7.

I was nearing the end. It was the middle of November. Astrid had come from Oslo and we went through the house together. I told her what I'd thrown away and what I'd kept. She had left it to me to clear things out, and now only the large items remained. It was a bitterly cold, windless day. A yellow wreath of stiffly frozen leaves lay on the ground under the ash tree; the few leaves that still remained on the branches gradually loosened and fell straight down. The sun had risen above the hills to the south, the rooms were bright and bare, and when I carried out the last boxes the gravel crunched under my shoes. We were in Josef's room when we heard the moving van drive into the yard.

"They're here now," I said.

The truck backed up all the way to the front steps, the ramp was lowered, and four men went with us into the living room.

Astrid and I had managed to push the piano out from the wall a little, perhaps as much as a meter, and now it was up to the movers to get it out of the house.

"It's heavy as lead," I said, as two men fastened straps on each side of the piano.

"No problem," one of the men replied. "As long as you've got straps, you can lift anything."

And it was true. They lifted simultaneously, and Mama's Steinway concert piano swayed between them. The last time it swung like that was in the spring of the first year of the war, when it was carried from the horse cart into the house. I saw the four deep grooves in the floor where it had stood for fifty-four years. The two men walked calmly, taking small steps, across the living room and through the door, holding on to the doorjambs, and then the final few meters out onto the front steps. There they put the piano on a dolly with rubber wheels, and after that it was just a matter of rolling it into the waiting van.

We had decided that Astrid would have the piano and I would have Herbert Andersson's painting, so the old concert piano set out on the four-hundred-kilometer journey back to Oslo, where at one time it stood in a basement apartment on Parkveien. The men secured it firmly in the truck, the hydraulic ramp went up, and soon they were ready to leave.

"It will probably have to be tuned when it arrives," one of the movers said.

Then they drove away.

I took the dented tin plates and Matiassen's lantern, Astrid took the picture of Jesus holding a lamb. I had already collected all of

Mama's clothes in large black garbage bags and delivered them to the meetinghouse, where they would be included in one of the annual trips to needy people in Russia. We divided the photo albums. Astrid got the three pictures of pregnant Mama in Oslo, since it was Astrid lying in Mama's stomach after all, while I got the caregiving papers: the contract for the five siblings, the settlement papers from Rebekka and Hertinius Olsen's estate, the letters I wrote to Josef and the siblings, and the final termination notice. We had divided everything of value, and at last all that remained was the bag of Tone's clothes.

"What are we going to do with them?" Astrid asked.

I gave her a questioning look.

"What do you think?" I said.

"You should have them," she replied. "You're the only one who remembers her."

At this time Astrid was forty-eight years old. She had some of Mama's features, especially her eyes and mouth. I saw that she also resembled Tone. When she looked at me I sometimes thought that it was Tone standing there, that this was what Tone would have been like: a woman of about fifty who reminded me of Mama and was waiting to hear what I'd say.

"I'll take them home with me," I said.

8.

It took another ten years after Papa died before Mama told me the rest of her story.

It was after her first stroke.

She lay looking at me with large, frightened eyes in the hospital on Tordenskjoldsgata in Kristiansand.

I was the one who found her. She was leaning back on the living room sofa at home. Half of her face was paralyzed, one corner of her mouth slid downward while the other half of her face was filled with terror. She stared at me open-mouthed, and I don't know how long she had sat like that, I don't know if she had tried to shout.

"Mama?" I said.

The ambulance arrived after forty-five minutes.

Meanwhile, I helped her lie down and propped up her head and neck with pillows; I asked if she wanted a glass of water, but didn't get a real reply. Her eyes were clear, however. She understood that she was unable to speak.

After several hours at the hospital the words gradually began to return, at first helter-skelter, as if everything was tossed around at random. Then the words seemed to find their way back to themselves, the sentences fell into place again, and in the course of a few days she spoke almost as before.

It was August 1994. They said it was a moderate stroke. No permanent paralysis. She had lost her speech, but it had come back.

A few days later she was transferred to the rest home in Nodeland, where Papa had been ten years earlier, but unlike him, she did not get worse, she continued to get better, and soon had improved enough to be able to go home.

I came to pick her up early one afternoon in the middle of August. For the first time, I noticed how thin she had become. Her light summer dress fluttered around her ankles when she stood up. She held on to the back of her chair, and the grass at her feet trembled.

"Have you come to get me?" she asked.

The fountain murmured softly. Several cars went by and continued north on the highway. I stood in front of her to block the sun.

"Yes, we're going home now," I replied.

She had difficulty with her balance, she who had always been so spry, running up and down the stairs at home with cups and containers and washtubs. Now she held my arm tightly. In my other hand I carried her suitcase, which was white and quite new. We walked like this over to the shade where my car was parked.

We drove the twenty kilometers home, and arrived sometime in the late afternoon. Our house stood just as it had since the war. Not much was changed after fifty years. The grass had grown freely this summer, and the branches of the ash tree stretched almost to what once had been Josef's window.

I helped her unfasten her seat belt, then we walked arm in arm across the yard. I found the key in her purse and let us into the house, where warm afternoon sunlight filled the front hall. After settling Mama on the sofa in the living room, I opened the windows wide to create a draft. The curtains blew inward, sheet music fluttered to the floor. I knew she had begun to play a little for herself after she was alone. I knew this, but never mentioned it.

I put on the coffeepot in the kitchen, turned on the radio on top of the refrigerator, and slowly the house came alive. The front hall, the living room, the kitchen—everything was the same: the low, blue-painted steps leading upstairs, the Steinway piano in the living room, the painting of Tone with the kitten in her arms. Time had stood still, but something had happened; Mama had suffered a stroke, I had picked her up at the rest home, and I didn't know how long I was going to stay.

It was a warm, pleasant afternoon, the sun still hung high above the pine-covered hills in the west, and after our meal I helped Mama out into the shade of the ash tree. Then I brought a chair from the kitchen and sat down with her.

There was a strange, cool stillness under the tree. It struck me that I'd never sat there before, exactly where Matiassen's stool always stood, even if perhaps I'd wanted to. We stayed maybe as long as an hour. I could see the roof and a little of the upstairs windows

down at Anna's house, but I didn't know if she was home, or if anyone had told her what had happened to Mama. We sat there as if in
the midst of a summer that was long past. I gazed across the fields,
at the woods, the sky. For the first time I saw everything Matiassen
must also have seen.

Sky. Clouds. Wind. Nothing.

It was then that she told me the rest.

She remembered the bronze lion, she remembered the Freia clock,
she remembered the Parliament building and the Royal Palace, she
remembered Foreign Ministry receptions held right above her head.
She remembered the laughter and singing and piano playing and
clinking of glasses into the wee hours of the night. She had decided to
get rid of the old suitcase, yet it remained in her room in the custodian apartment. She had decided to cut her hair short, but instead she
lay in bed for several days. Grandpa took care of her as best he could,
but she felt terrible.

She was four months pregnant.

She wrote a letter to Papa saying that perhaps she couldn't bear
to come back. But as soon as she mailed the letter, she wrote another one saying that she wasn't sure.

How can I sleep in the bed where Tone died?

That was the question.

Papa wrote in return, but I don't know how he responded. Their
letters had gone back and forth during the fall, and when once
again she stood in the Vestbanen station waiting for the train to
Stavanger, she was wearing a new dress that fit her stomach better, her hair had grown longer, and next to her was the suitcase that
had been with her for two births and when they moved to southern Norway.

That was the story.

She kept the old suitcase, she did not cut her hair. She did not
start over again, but Grandpa gave her a new dress that wasn't so

tight at the waist. She sat in the train on her way back. Through the window she saw the broad fields when the train neared Drammen, she saw the same distant mountain ridges she had seen from Dikemark. Sunlight glittered on the sea around the cargo boats, and in Kongsberg the bridge over the Lågen River had been rebuilt and the train glided slowly across it to the other side.

I didn't ask what Papa had written; maybe I thought I'd ask later, but at that moment I let it be. Instead, I asked about Cain and Abel.

"What happened to the two kittens?" I asked.

Mama looked at me.

"Don't you know?" she said.

"No."

"He killed them. Papa killed them."

We sat in our chairs gazing at the landscape until the sun sank so low that the insects began to flare up overhead, and finally Mama grew so tired I had to help her into the house.

That was when I carried her.

She put her arm around my shoulders, I picked her up, and we walked through the grass toward the front steps and the open door like a newly married couple. It was the first and only time I carried her. She was much lighter than I had imagined. For some reason I'd thought she would be heavy. I'd thought I wouldn't be able to carry her. But the moment she put her arm around my neck I knew it would be just fine. I sensed at once how light she was; I sensed the bones in her thighs, the ribs under her blouse, the fragrance of her hair; I sensed how little was left of her. I walked through the grass with Mama in my arms, and I was the bridegroom carrying his bride into the house. Fourteen days later she had a second, massive stroke. Fourteen days later she was dead. I thought she would be heavy, as if I were still a child, as if part of me was still a child. Or perhaps I'd been given unexpected strength. Because at the time it felt as if I could carry her anywhere, no matter where it might be; I could have continued down the road, past the hawthorn hedge and Anna's house, to the roadside milk platform, across the valley and the bridge over the Djupåna River, past the meetinghouse and the vacant store with its balcony above the road. I could have just kept walking, and it would have been as if I carried nothing in my arms.

PART FIVE

1.

For some reason my letters to Josef and the siblings lay with the caregiving papers. Mama must have saved them and put them aside. I thought I'd written many letters home, but there were only six in the writing desk. I recognized my handwriting, I saw the dates and postmarks, I remembered the view from the different rooms where I'd written the letters, but I did not remember anything of what I wrote.

I had the feeling that the letters were written to me.

In the fall of 1952 I wrote to Ingrid, Erling, and Josef for the first time. The letter was postmarked Kvås. I remember that I sat alone in my dormitory room, the window looked out on green spaces, the Lygna River sparkled, and I remember feeling far away from home.

The next letter was postmarked Heistadmoen military base. I wrote about life in the camp, about being issued a uniform and a beret, and I promised to come home for a visit as soon as I got my first leave.

Which I did.

I stood in the front hall at home in my new off-duty uniform. Josef had put on his uniform jacket for the occasion; he wore the medal for courage on his chest and had the Border Resident card in his pocket. I let him borrow my beret, and Ingrid was allowed to gently touch the buttons on my uniform. As we stood there, Mama came out from the kitchen. My hair had been cut very short and I was quite unrecognizable I'm sure. She dried her hands on her apron.

"Is it you?" she asked.

There was one more letter from my years in the military, this time from Porsanger garrison in Finnmark:

Dear everyone at home,

I'm in Porsanger now, about as far north as it is possible to go in Norway. It's light the whole night here, and there are lots of mosquitoes. I'll be here a couple of months, before I'm sent south again. Hope you are all fine there at home. I understand you have good weather this summer in southern Norway too. I've been to the Russian border. I stood high up in a watchtower and looked into Russia, but seen from the air Russia is not very different from Norway. That's all for now. I'll write again when I'm coming home. Greet Mama and Papa. Take care!

PS: Now it's not only Josef who has seen the midnight sun!

I left the parish in southern Norway, just like Papa, and completed basic training and military academy for noncommissioned officers. But then, instead of going to Oslo and Diakonhjemmet like Papa did, I went back to southern Norway, to Kristiansand and the teachers college close to Oddernes church. Every day I sat in the old classrooms with a view across the European Highway toward the whitewashed stone church and surrounding cemetery. I rented a studio apartment near Gimlemoen military base, and in the evenings I could see the lights of the old Eg asylum reflected in the river. I saw the pointed church steeple jutting up from the grounds of the asylum, the same steeple that both Christian Jensen and Matiassen must have seen at one time.

Now and then I heard the faint clang of the church bell. The sound just barely carried across the water.

I was going to be a teacher, like Nils Apesland, but I did not have any grass snakes in my pockets, I did not skid down Gaustatoppen Mountain on the soles of my shoes, and when my final exam was over I did not go home on foot.

Instead I wrote another letter to Ingrid, Erling, Nils, Sverre, Lilly, and Josef. I sat by an open window in my little apartment, where I'd just given notice. It was early summer, in the garden the apple trees were blooming; I saw seagulls circling a small fishing boat headed up the river; I heard occasional traffic over the Lundsbrua Bridge. I smelled the sea.

I wrote that I was getting married.

I wrote that I had met a girl at the teachers college, that we had noticed each other from the very beginning, but only now when we had completed our education, early summer 1963, had we decided to get married. The letter was mostly about me. I realized this at the time. And I realized it more than thirty years later when I read the letter again. Everything was about me. I remember I folded the letter, put it in an envelope, and addressed it. Then I took a summer evening stroll to the red mailbox outside the venerable main residence at Gimlemoen. I imagined Ingrid's face when Josef read my letter. I imagined she would howl softly and pleasantly, or perhaps she would howl painfully. Suddenly I saw her in my mind. She was howling painfully.

I got married that September.

In December I wrote a Christmas card, but didn't mention that I would become a father the following year. I didn't write anything when my son was born, in July 1964. No one, neither Josef nor the siblings, knew I'd become a father until September of that year, when we had the baptism at home. During the party afterward, I went upstairs to see Lilly and Ingrid with the little boy in my arms. I knocked softly, and heard light footsteps inside. The door opened and Lilly stood there staring at me.

"Is it you?" she said.

"Yes, of course," I said. "I'm not alone, as you can see. May we come in?"

Lilly moved aside, Ingrid got up from the table, and I took a few steps into the room with the baby in my arms.

"Who's that?" said Lilly, pointing to the baby.

"This is my son," I replied. "He was baptized today."

"Your son?"

"Yes indeed."

"You have a son?"

"Yes," I replied again. "He's still a tiny baby."

Lilly looked at me, then at the boy.

"What's his name?"

I said his name, and then Ingrid wanted to see too.

"Look, Ingrid," I said. "I have a son."

Ingrid was silent. Lilly had no further questions.

"Look," I said. "Isn't he tiny?"

Ingrid nodded. She gradually came closer.

"Do you want to hold him?"

We sat down on Ingrid's bed, all three of us, and I placed the sleeping baby in Ingrid's lap. She regarded him silently with a serious expression. Though she seemed uncomfortable, she held him almost naturally. She drooled a little, as she always did. And then she howled, softly and pleasantly. Finally I picked up the baby and laid him in Lilly's lap. Like her sister, she held him almost naturally, almost effortlessly. The little boy was asleep; Lilly looked at him, then at me and at Ingrid. After a while she said:

"You can take him now."

I took the baby gently from her lap. He had slept soundly the whole time, but when he was back in my arms he woke up. He lay with his eyes wide open, gazing at me.

2.

I continued to write letters home. I had gotten a teaching position at Oddemarka school in Kristiansand, and wrote about small, every-day events, harmless things: about a novel I'd read, about unruly students, about the seagulls that glided in the wind outside my window. I wrote to Nils, Erling, and Sverre at the Nærlandsheimen address, and always received an answer telling me that the letter had been read aloud to the brothers. During the World Ski Championship in 1966 I wrote to Josef about Bjørn Wirkola, who jumped farther than everyone, because I knew Josef would empathize especially with *that*.

After all, I knew about Josef's own ski jumping.

Then, in the summer of 1967, I wrote that we were going to move back to my old parish. I'd gotten a job at the central school in Lauvlandsmoen, and we were going to build a house about halfway between the meetinghouse and my childhood home. Like Papa, I moved back home and built a house.

The letter was postmarked June 17, 1967. It was the last one.

That's how I happened to return. Fifteen years had passed. We moved into our new house just before Christmas. The area was the same, the people were the same, Reinert was still the parish clerk and sexton. Still, there were changes. The public library had moved a hundred meters from Dr. Rosenvold's old office, beyond the meetinghouse to the second floor of the town hall, right above the bank. Moreover, the doctor's office had been turned into a garage. During the past seventeen years Josef had managed to get through the library's entire collection a few times, but the number of books had increased during the sixties, so he made progress more slowly.

"Not more authors beginning with D!" he complained.

He had become an old man.

One evening I picked up Josef, Lilly, and Ingrid and drove them to our new house.

"You're going to live here?" Lilly asked, as she entered the front hall.

"Yes, that's what we plan to do," I replied. "That will be nice, don't you think?"

"Yes, that will be nice," she said reflectively.

I showed Ingrid around the house: the living room, the kitchen, the baby's room. After that, we made a short visit to the garden. It was dark, starlit, very cold; her hand, too, was very cold. When we came in, Lilly and Josef were waiting with their coats on, ready to leave.

"Will you give us a ride home in your carriage?" Josef asked.

"Yes indeed," I replied.

We stood for a moment on the lighted porch. I saw how old Josef had become. Lilly had also grown older. Ingrid as well. We had all gotten older. I shut the door behind us, and we walked in the dark toward the car.

Tone would have been twenty-seven years old.

3.

The parish was the same, the people were the same, but upstairs great changes had taken place. After Matiassen was taken to Heslandsheimen in the winter of 1962, Nils, Sverre, and Erling moved into his old room, while Ingrid and Lilly remained together. It was a natural arrangement. The boys by themselves, the girls by themselves. For a long time things seemed to go well. However, Erling constantly suffered from severe headaches, migraines perhaps. Frequently he was confined to bed. Often with both hands pressed against his ears. Sometimes he wrapped his blanket around his head and lay like that, as if a spider had spun a cocoon around its egg. He regularly had to listen to his two brothers squabbling. And at times he was seized by powerful rage; he tore off his blanket and pounded his hand against the wall, hard, again and again. But only once did the brothers start to fight.

They heard the screams from far away, and when Papa went upstairs the three brothers were struggling with each other on the floor. Tables, chairs, every loose object, had been strewn around. One windowpane was smashed, Sverre had cut his hand, Nils clutched a broken chair leg in his fist. Erling screamed and screamed, saliva ran from his mouth; his howls were heartbreaking, and he didn't calm down until Lilly came in and put his head in her lap.

Later no one could explain how the fight started, but after a while Erling moved back with his sisters, while Sverre and Nils stayed in Matiassen's room. Things went on like that for a few months. It was a game of solitaire that couldn't be won. Sverre slowly changed from a quiet, timid four-year-old into a rebellious young man. His hair was long and wiry, his eyes a striking clear blue. From a distance one certainly could not tell that he was mentally disabled. He refused to have his hair cut. When Papa came with the scissors, Sverre might knock his head against the wall or on the table. He would bang his head so hard the tin plates bounced. During meals he might suddenly sweep aside his cutlery and drinking glass and thump his head on the table, hard, hard, while Lilly screamed and Erling laughed and Nils stood up with his plate in his hand. Or he might decide to run away. Suddenly he would slam his fork on the table and dash down the stairs, out to the yard, and into the woods. Papa had to lock the front door while they ate, and eventually also while they slept. Sverre might decide to sneak out in the middle of the night. First he set off silently across the room and down the stairs, then he began to run, even though it was pitch black outside, even though he knew he would not find the way back by himself. He wasn't afraid, he knew someone always came to find him. He ran into the forest or down the road past Hans and Anna's house toward Brandsvoll, and maybe even farther, shouting and screaming and waking the neighbors. He didn't know where he was, but he knew someone would always find him. As long as he screamed, someone would always find him.

It became impossible in the long run. They couldn't watch him around the clock. Finally, they'd had enough.

Papa wrote to the Child Welfare office in Stavanger to ask about possible care facilities for Sverre, and perhaps for Erling and Nils as well, perhaps for all three brothers together. They had become grown men after all; they had lived together their entire lives, and maybe the time had come for a change.

After several weeks an answer arrived from Stavanger; the letter stated in black and white that Nils, Sverre, and Erling had been accepted at Nærlandsheimen, outside Nærbø, in Jæren.

For now, just the three brothers.

That evening Mama and Papa went upstairs to tell everyone the big news. Papa knocked on the door, and Lilly opened it.

"Is it you?" she said.

"We have something to tell you," said Papa. "May we come in?"

Lilly gathered all the siblings around the table. They sat there as they had for almost twenty years, while Papa told them about the place near the sea where Nils and Sverre and Erling were going to live now.

"You will each have your own room and your own bed," he said.

"Will we get food?" asked Nils.

"As much as you can eat," said Mama.

There was a slight pause. Nils grinned. Erling seemed restless, his head wobbled back and forth. Mama went over and placed her hand gently on his shoulder, and at that moment he suddenly began to clap his hands enthusiastically. Erling clapped, then Sverre began to clap, then Ingrid and Lilly and Nils, and so the short conversation about the place near the sea ended with long, hearty applause.

4.

The three brothers left on a cold morning in November. Papa would drive them to Marnardal station; from there, three nurses, who had boarded the train in Kristiansand, would go with them to Jæren. The three left without ceremony. Nils was allowed to ride in the front seat of the Ambassador and he triumphantly waved from the side window to his sisters, who remained behind. The car headed down the road, turned left by the milk platform, and disappeared.

A new era began.

Together with forty other boys and men from all parts of the country, Nils, Erling, and Sverre moved into a brand-new building for *asocial, mentally disabled men* located in Nærbø, a few hundred meters from the seashore. Each got his own room, with a view of the ocean from the window. It was not far from Stavanger, where they had once lived, so it was almost like moving back home. Or perhaps they had forgotten everything that happened before they came to us. Perhaps they had forgotten that they had lived anywhere but with us.

At any rate, *to come home* meant to come back to the big house in the middle of the woods, forty kilometers from the coast.

Every year in mid-December, Mama and Papa stood on the platform at Marnardal station waiting for the train from Stavanger, which had stopped at Nærbø to pick up about ten patients, all going south to celebrate Christmas with their families. The Christmas tree in the square outside the train station was laden with snow, almost like the tree in the yard outside Dikemark in Papa's youth. A dense December darkness had fallen, snowflakes swirled under the yellow station lights. They heard the train whistle in the distance and moved closer to the tracks. Soon the locomotive came thundering into the station in a cloud of snow with a string of cars behind it. Mama and Papa waited calmly as the platform filled with travelers, and when Nils, Erling, and Sverre climbed out of the last car it must have felt almost like having their children home. Erling laughed, Nils shook Papa's hand, and Sverre had become gentle and peaceful. Perhaps he was on medication.

When the brothers came home, the house immediately grew lively. Mama had gotten their old room ready; the beds were made, Christmas curtains hung in the windows. The three had much to tell after months in the large building far to the west by the sea. Nils and Sverre talked at the same time, Erling laughed with his hands on his ears, and at night Lilly prayed a short evening prayer with them before they could all go to sleep.

They sang "Blessed Lord."

They still had childlike voices.

On Christmas Eve, I came with my family, Astrid had arrived from Oslo, and we celebrated Christmas together as in the past. Josef stood by the piano, and only the one lamp was lit. Strictly speaking, he sang only on *the Big Day*, but he made another exception. He sang as he always did: in a loud voice, with fine, clear articulation. He looked like a cultivated elderly nobleman as he stood there in the soft light, and afterward he got tremendous applause. Erling and Sverre clapped and clapped, and Josef bowed with his hand on his stomach.

"Merci," he said. "Au revoir."

The five siblings ate and sang and opened Christmas presents that Mama and Papa had bought for them. They received mittens and scarves and small marzipan pigs that Lilly gathered up for safekeeping. New Year's Eve we celebrated together again. We sat in front of the television and watched the king's New Year speech from the Royal Palace in Oslo. Everyone was silent. The king spoke. We let the words sink in. Afterward, Papa went out into the yard with his Mauser rifle on his shoulder, while the rest of us stood waiting by the windows. It was very dark outside. We saw nothing but a reflection of the living room and our own white faces, but we all knew Papa was out there, and we all knew what was going to happen. Erling and Ingrid covered their ears, Sverre dozed, and Nils grinned the way he always did. Suddenly there was a loud bang. Erling laughed wildly, waving his arms, and hid his head in his sweater; Ingrid howled and hung on to Sverre. Five more bangs echoed back and forth among the hills like the sound of English fighter planes, and then the new year could begin.

5.

There were days with sunshine and drifting clouds, there were evenings with rain from the southwest and misty mornings when the pine trees were barely visible. Not completely dark, but still not light enough to distinguish the closest trees from the rest of the forest. The ash tree motionless. Easter lilies in the garden, like small white bonfires scattered in an unknown shadowland.

Suddenly it was autumn.

On November 25, 1965, Rebekka Olsen died in a nursing home in Stavanger. Two years later, on October 14, 1967, stonemason Hertinius Olsen followed her to the grave.

None of their five mentally disabled children were with them.

The parents had visited the children just once. It had gone well. Fifteen years passed, and then both parents were dead.

I don't know what Rebekka felt that day in late December 1944 when Inspector Aarrestad from the Child Welfare office stood in the miserable apartment near Strandgata surrounded by her filthy children.

Perhaps she felt ashamed.

Perhaps she felt like an old woman.

Several weeks after Hertinius died, an inventory of the estate was made, and later a meeting was held regarding the beneficiaries. The estate's assets were found to be a good fifteen thousand *kroner* in cash. Liabilities included a number of expenses in connection with settling the estate: government taxes of three hundred *kroner* and eighty-three *øre*, a registration fee of twenty *kroner*. Various probate court expenses, nine *kroner* for deponents with cars, plus fifty *kroner* for the death certificate filled out by district medical officer Håberg.

A total of nine items. People made sure they got paid.

Finally, a thousand *kroner* were set aside to pay for a common gravestone for the couple.

When everything was deducted, the inheritance had shrunk to thirteen thousand four hundred forty-nine *kroner* and thirty-one *øre*. Divided by five.

Papa went upstairs with the money that came to Lilly and Ingrid, two thousand six hundred eighty-nine *kroner* for each, carefully counted out and placed in two brown envelopes. Ingrid ripped open her envelope with her thumb, emptied the money on the table, and watched in amazement as the *kroner* coins and fifty-*øre* pieces rolled across the floor and under the bed. Lilly took her envelope without opening it, but she made a deep, dignified curtsy as always. And rightly so at last. Suddenly she had become wealthy. A package of Gjende shortbread cost no more than a couple of *kroner* at the Brandsvoll store, a bottle of Asina could not be much more, and she no longer needed to sell dried flowers.

Every Sunday they counted the money. The house was Sunday quiet; Josef and Papa were at church, Mama was down in the kitchen preparing dinner for everyone. Ingrid stacked the coins in crooked piles, and there was never a single øre missing.

They had nothing to spare for the missionaries.

Papa set up a joint account at the savings bank located in the new Brandsvoll town hall, and one day the three of them took the money there. They stood at the counter, each sister with her envelope; the teller opened the little window and was going to take the money, but Lilly suddenly would not give up her envelope.

"It's my money," she said.

"We can take care of it for you," said the teller. "And then you'll have even more money."

"I don't believe it," said Lilly.

With that she turned and walked away.

In the end they went home again with the money. They had a joint account at the savings bank, but the money lay in the brown envelopes in their room. All through the years, the account remained empty.

6.

Josef managed to read all the books in the public library seven or eight times, according to his count. That did not include the poetry books, and perhaps also Ibsen's plays. He must have been one of the most well-read people in the parish, but whether he remembered anything from all those books was another matter. He was also among the most faithful churchgoers. Now and then he walked alone the five kilometers to church. Occasionally he got lost, but someone always found him along the road and guided him in the right direction. He had his regular place in church, in the front row on the right, with a good view of the altar rail and the pulpit with three evangelists painted on it. He saw four parish pastors come and go, but the sexton, Reinert Sløgedal, was there the entire time. Sløgedal was the same, and Anna at the reed organ was the same. Anna glanced at the organ mirror, Josef sang louder than everyone else, and if by chance the former sheriff was in church on Sunday, Josef did his best to talk with him and stand shoulder to shoulder with him in the churchyard.

Everyone knew Josef. And Josef knew everyone.

As the winters went by, he became a regular participant in the annual so-called graybeard ski jumping meet at Buåsjordet, halfway between Brandsvoll and Breivoll. The meet was held in March, the snow was sticky, and most entrants were very mature men. Josef was helped with his skis, and then lifted into place in the tracks while two men held his arms.

"Are you ready, Josef?" came the shout from below.

"Josef is ready!" he shouted.

They let him go, and Josef whizzed down toward the end of the inrun. The tips of his skis trembled, people held their breath. Long before the end of the inrun Josef took off for a leap. He flew through the air like a strange bird, leaving his cap lying on the inrun, and at the end he landed smack on the outrun with his skis and poles in every direction.

That's how it usually went.

However, one time a miracle occurred. It was a winter in the late fifties. Josef was placed in the ski tracks as usual, they let him go, he whooshed down, took off for the leap, flew through the air flapping his arms wildly. And landed on his feet. It was as if he didn't really understand what had happened. His cap lay on the inrun, but he had landed on his feet, and he stayed upright all the way to the finish.

Afterward he was interviewed by Reinert Sløgedal, who was a reporter for the event. Josef's jump was measured to be three meters and seventy-five centimeters, with the landing, and Sløgedal asked what had been the most difficult: the inrun, the flight, or the landing.

Josef considered the question for a moment, and then replied: "The flight, of course. The flight."

It must have been one of the great moments in his life. The time he landed on his feet, and then Sløgedal's interview, which was printed afterward in the athletic club's annual report. Later he would forget all the times he had fallen. Later it was only this one jump that counted.

He received a small cup as a prize, and when he came home he put it on the windowsill in his room. The cup must have been silver because it constantly turned black and had to be polished, but then it became so glossy you could see yourself in it. Josef always took the cup with him to church and to the store, and later he had it with him when he visited his sister in Tønsberg for summer vacation each year. After a while he just called it *the wandering cup*.

Yes, he had a sister in Tønsberg.

She had been essentially absent his whole life, until one summer day in 1968 Josef received a letter in the mail. That was very unusual. Papa came upstairs with the large, sealed envelope.

"Letter for Mr. Josef," he said.

Josef stood up

"For me?" he said in surprise.

Papa handed him the envelope.

"This must be from the king!" Josef exclaimed, as he ripped open the seal.

It wasn't from the king, but from his sister in Tønsberg. She wrote to tell him about a sum of money he should have received in 1936, the year their father died; at the time she had been in a difficult situation, however, and needed to borrow his part of the inheritance for a while. The years had gone by. More precisely, thirty-two years and four months, and now she was finally able to pay back the loan. Warm greetings. A check for eighteen hundred *kroner* enclosed.

After all, it had just been a loan.

Suddenly Josef was wealthy, like Ingrid and Lilly, but in contrast to them, he had no doubt about how the money should be used. One day he and Papa went to Kristiansand, where Josef bought a brand-new Telefunken television in a teak cabinet with sliding doors in front of the screen.

Every evening Josef opened the sliding doors, turned on the television set, waited until the picture appeared, then sat down on a chair in the middle of the room and watched programs until the broadcasts were over for the evening.

He had become rich, he had his own television set, the big, black-and-white world came right into his room, the wandering cup stood on the windowsill, he received good food, and had a warm bed. He had lost the Border Resident card with a broadly smiling picture of himself, but he could see his face and smile reflected in the wandering cup, just like in the medal for courage. He could hold up the cup with a big smile. His smile was slightly distorted in the silver.

Sometimes Lilly sat there with him. She heard when he opened the sliding doors and turned the knob. After a few minutes she came in quietly and sat down at the very edge of the bed, as if she were afraid she would be told to leave.

Perhaps it was sort of a love affair.

After all, they had gone to Lake Djupesland together once, but what happened there, nobody knew. Maybe he had touched her arm. Maybe a bird had been perched on the sandbar. In any case, she had started to scream.

A love affair perhaps, but if so, almost without a word, almost without exchanging a glance, perhaps also without touching.

They sat staring at the images that flickered across the screen and lit up their faces. Now and then Ingrid sat with them, quiet and shy, as if she too were afraid she would be told to leave.

Josef's mustache twitched, and he cleared his throat as if he planned to say something—something definitive that he had thought about for a long time. A comment about what they saw. Or perhaps something he wanted to say to Lilly. But he only cleared his throat. He didn't say anything. Perhaps it was Lilly he had seen under the midnight sun in Trondheim, perhaps she was the young bride. At long last they were reunited.

Their favorite program was *Krutrøyk*.

If there was a parliamentary election, they watched the election broadcasts in September. They watched the daily news each evening at seven-thirty, and usually children's television at six too. Sometimes they laughed heartily. The laughter could be heard outside in the spring evening. If it could be called laughter. They saw when Martin Luther King Jr. was murdered in Memphis. They saw the first Soviet tanks roll through the streets of Prague. They saw Crown Prince Harald marry his Sonja Haraldsen in the Oslo Cathedral. They sat without moving and just watched. Without a word. They saw the newly married couple come out into the sunlight on the palace balcony and wave to the people.

7.

Time flowed on, in Josef's life too, even though in a way he always stayed the same. He was somehow a child. His hair was white, as was his mustache. An old, very well-read child.

Just before Christmas in 1968, *Apollo 8* circled the moon.

Another spring arrived, another summer, another fall.

The leaves loosened and fell from the ash tree, leaving the branches black against the sky.

On November 16, 1969, Josef turned seventy-seven.

November 21 was a Friday. Calm, mild late-autumn weather. After reading in his room the whole morning, Josef suddenly decided to take a walk to the rifle range in Hønemyr. It was about two kilometers, the same route I had taken back and forth to school. He met Mama on the stairs. They exchanged a few words about the weather, and he told her where he was going; then he put on his uniform jacket and a cap, and left. Out in the yard he met Papa. They also talked about the weather, and when Josef started down the road Papa stood on the front steps and watched him disappear around the bend.

He's gotten old, Papa said to himself.

In all likelihood Josef walked all the way to the rifle range in Hønemyr. Maybe he sat down for a while in the pale November sunshine outside the shooting lodge before walking home. Maybe he thought about the midnight sun above Trondheim. Maybe he thought about his young bride waiting for him at home.

He was gone for a long time.

Around three o'clock, it started to get dark.

At first they thought he had gotten lost; that had happened before, after all. But this time he had said he would stay on the road, and then he always found his way home again, or somebody found *him* and telephoned. And that was exactly what happened. Papa was on his way out the door to look for him when the telephone rang in the front hall. It was Tilla Båsland. She said just two words: *It's Josef.*

Tilla was busy preparing boiled potatoes when she happened to look out the window and saw a man squatting in the middle of the road. He sat like a Bedouin in the desert, perhaps twenty meters from the house. At first she was frightened. She went into her living room and looked out the window that faced east. Then she realized who it was. By the time she got outside, Josef had collapsed even further. He sat as if he had fallen straight down from heaven and landed in the middle of the road, and when she put a hand on his shoulder it was almost as if he were asleep.

Josef sat there in the twilight wrapped in a blanket when I drove up in my car. In the bright beam of the headlights I could see him clearly, but I don't think he realized what was happening around him. I waited behind the wheel while Jon, Tilla, and Papa helped him into the backseat.

"I'm going to drive you home now, Josef," I said over my shoulder.

But Josef did not reply. Papa got in next to Josef, and in the rearview mirror I saw Josef's head flop down on Papa's shoulder. I sped the few hundred meters back home and stopped outside the front door, where Mama stood waiting. Papa and I helped Josef inside. We realized what was happening. Lilly stood at the top of the stairs, and when she saw Josef she was terrified; she put her hands over her mouth, and ran back to be with Ingrid. We got to Josef's room. Papa wanted to remove the uniform jacket, but Josef revived a little and refused to take off anything. His shoes were the only things we were allowed to touch, and then the whole world could see that he had forgotten to put on socks. He lay there barefoot in his uniform jacket while Mama telephoned the district doctor in Nodeland. I stood in his room, where I'd so often sat on the wood box with Ingrid, Erling, or Tone. This time I wanted to say something, but I didn't know what to say. I just stood there and watched as Josef became increasingly pale, his breath weaker. His hair was very white against the pillow, and his mustache looked like a rumpled feather that had landed just above his mouth. The wandering cup on the windowsill was bluish-black. It hadn't been polished for a long time.

When Mama came up, he seemed to revive in spite of everything. He opened his eyes and looked at her.

"The doctor is on his way, Josef," she said.

"Rosenvold?" Josef said.

"No," said Mama. "There's another doctor now."

Josef asked to have an extra pillow behind his back, and as he sat there propped up in bed we heard his voice:

"Am I going to die now?"

I don't know how Mama replied. I don't know if she said anything at all, but I don't think Josef meant it as a question.

"Can I have a hug, my dear little Karin?" he said. At first Mama just stood there. Then she leaned over and put her arms around him, and when she straightened up Uncle Josef was dead.

8.

Anna played for the funeral, as she had for Tone's funeral, and for the Christmas concert. The first snow had fallen, and the woodstove with its long stovepipe had been exchanged for electric heaters that crackled under the pews. We were all there: Mama and Papa, Lilly and Ingrid, Astrid and I. Sverre, Erling, and Nils had come by train all the way from Nærbø.

The church was filled. Even the balconies.

Arne Nicolay Kvellestad officiated.

When Kvellestad talked about Josef's life, at times the congregation broke into subdued, kindly laughter. He described the visit and guided tour the year before, and he told about Josef singing each year on his birthday, and how he had flown through the air at Buåsjordet, landed on his feet, and stayed upright all the way to the finish.

"This is the ski jump that will remain in our memories," said Kvellestad.

Then he repeated what Josef had said in the interview with the reporter Sløgedal when asked what was most difficult—the inrun, the flight, or the landing.

"The flight," Josef had said. "The flight."

Afterward, when Anna played "Joyful, Joyful," Papa bent forward. He rubbed his hands up and down his face as if he were trying to tear it off. Then he leaned his forehead against the pew in front of us, and for the first and last time in my life I saw him weep.

That was how Josef's strange life ended. He had flapped through the air, but landed on his feet. He'd read world literature and attended church services. He had seen his reflection in the medal of courage, and later in the wandering cup.

I think that was enough.

What no one knew was that Josef would be buried next to Sheriff Kristen Lauvsland, who died only three weeks later, in mid-December 1969. For all eternity Josef would lie shoulder to shoulder with the sheriff himself. Not even in his dreams could he have imagined such an honor. Not in his wildest fantasies. That must have been the greatest reward and triumph that life—and finally death—could have given him.

9.

One summer day in 1973 Papa telephoned me to say he had terminated the caregiving agreement for Lilly and Ingrid. I don't recall exactly what was said in our brief conversation, but he told me about the letter he had written to the Stavanger Social Services office, about Johannessen and Håberg's visit, and about the answer he had received. I remember his voice. He sounded weary.

For now, only Ingrid would move to Nærlandsheimen; she had been given a place there, like her three brothers, but Lilly still had to live at home until a place was found for her too. Perhaps at Nærlandsheimen, perhaps at Bakkebø in Egersund. Perhaps somewhere else. One didn't know.

The time had come for the move, and Papa wanted me to make the trip west with them. He thought that Ingrid might be difficult, and that I might somehow be able to convince her, or at least calm her down.

After all, at one time we were almost siblings.

I drove across the open countryside near Brandsvoll, turned right and crossed the Djupåna River, continued past Sløgedal's home and up to the house at the edge of the woods. The calm, bright summer morning made me feel lighthearted; it was the kind of morning I had so often experienced as a child. It was cool in the shade of the ash tree. Papa stood there waiting for me.

We had agreed that Lilly would come along. We planned not to say anything until the actual time. We would all drive west, but only Ingrid would remain at Nærlandsheimen, although neither of the sisters knew that.

Papa strolled around the yard with his hands in his pockets as he whistled a tune with no beginning or end. Lilly stood with a suitcase on the top step outside; Ingrid came out behind her, shading her eyes from the sun.

"Well, well," said Papa cheerfully. "So you're all set."

I took the suitcase and put it in the trunk. Mama went around checking that all the doors were closed and locked, while Lilly and Ingrid followed right behind her. The three of them left dark tracks in the dewy grass. Lilly wore a gray coat belted at the waist and a flowered shawl over her shoulders; the coat was so long that it got wet at the bottom.

Mama went up the hay barn bridge to make sure the door was locked properly, then Lilly went to check, and Ingrid did exactly the same. After that Mama checked to see that the cattle barn door was locked, and that the hook on the old outhouse was fastened properly. Lilly waited behind her, as if for her turn, and then she did the same thing.

"All locked," said Lilly.

Mama put the house key under the doormat, and we were ready to leave.

At that point, Ingrid refused to get into the car.

Papa held the door open for her, but she just stood there and refused to budge. She howled softly, and as I sat behind the steering wheel I heard it was painful howling. I was afraid of what would happen if I turned around and looked at her. Maybe she sensed what was happening, maybe she'd had suspicions.

Finally, I got out of the car. Without hesitating for a moment, I went over to Ingrid and took her hand.

"Come, Ingrid," I said. "Come, let's take a little walk."

So we walked around the house again. I took a chance, and had no idea what would happen. I led her through the warm morning sunshine and into the cool shade behind the house. She no longer howled, she grew very calm; her hand was soft. We walked without saying a word. When we came back into the sunshine I saw our shadows, which had merged into one long black figure that glided across the grass beside us.

"One more time?" I asked.

She nodded.

After walking around the house again, I led Ingrid over to the car, and she sat down in the backseat next to Lilly as if nothing had happened.

Mama and Papa were already waiting in the car. I started the engine, and we drove past the hawthorn hedge, down the road to the milk platform and mailboxes; there the road curved left, I increased our speed, and we continued up a gentle slope. If Ingrid and Lilly had turned around at that moment they would have seen our house for the last time. We passed Sløgedal's garden and, on the left-hand side, the new fire station surrounded by pine forest. Soon we crossed the Djupåna River, and at the crossroads I turned left again. It was the same route that Lilly and Ingrid took when they went to the store to buy Asina and Gjende shortbread. The walk home used to take just long enough for them to eat all the shortbread, but now they hardly had a chance to think before we were beyond the store. Besides, the store had been shut down and turned into a stable; the only thing unchanged was the elegant, but now disintegrating, balcony that hung out over the road. I remembered the day we arrived, over thirty years ago, when the bus stopped there and I dreamed of looking out from the balcony. I remembered how Papa stopped whistling when we approached our house for the first time.

As I signaled a right turn and put on the brakes for a moment, I heard Lilly's voice:

"Are we there soon?"

We drove west across Lauvslandsmoen, passed the new central school, and crossed the bridge over the Finsåna River, where the water was barely flowing now in the middle of summer. At the highest point on the road, we saw blue uplands stretching westward toward Audnedal, and at that moment, Lilly and Ingrid left the parish for good.

We came to Nærbø in the early afternoon, and followed the signs for Nærlandsheimen. I turned left onto a narrow gravel road running parallel to a stone fence that led straight to the sea.

Nærlandsheimen actually consisted of numerous buildings. At one time Diakonhjemmet in Oslo had bought the property for the purpose of building a *work-and-care facility for the mentally disabled* where a *Christlike spirit of love* was translated into action. At first it consisted only of the so-called Stone House, but through the decades more and more structures had been built. In addition to the white administration building, there were others of various sizes spread out over a large area; in the middle was the redbrick Stefanus church, named after the first Christian martyr, the patron saint of weavers, coachmen—and stonemasons.

I parked by the administration building and got out of the car after the long trip. It was chilly, almost cold; I smelled the fresh tang of the sea, but could not see the water from where we stood. Ingrid got out. Lilly got out. I looked for Erling, Nils, and Sverre, but there was no one to be seen.

"Where is this?" Lilly asked.

We all waited while Papa went in to say we had arrived. I got my jacket from the car.

"We're there now," said Mama.

The director of Nærlandsheimen gave us a tour. He showed us where the American Telegraph office had been housed until the telegraph poles were torn down and moved to Jeløya Island, in the Oslo Fjord; he showed us the new building for social worker training, and the tower that pumped seawater into a new indoor swimming pool; he showed us Stefanus church, which had been consecrated by the bishop in 1969, and the athletic field, which had been inaugurated with a soccer game between Nærlandsheimen and Bakkebø. We heard the whole history of Nærlandsheimen, from its opening in 1948, to the many additions through the years, until the day in July 1973 when we stood outside the Stone House and looked at everything.

It was an impressive institution, with almost one thousand employees. There were two bells in the Stefanus church tower. Engraved on one were these words: *God wants me to be a happy child.*

Finally we were shown Erling's, Nils's, and Sverre's rooms, which were still in the building for asocial, mentally disabled men. Then we were led down a long corridor with closed doors on each side; at the far end was a spacious lounge with large windows facing the sea, and there they were, all three. It was strange to see them in unfamiliar surroundings. For thirty years I had been used to their living upstairs at home. The voices through the floor, the table grace before meals. The feeling didn't let go. They really belonged with us.

"So this is where you live," I said.

"Yeah, yeah, by George," said Nils.

We all sat there looking at the view, for perhaps as long as fifteen minutes. And Lilly was calm, in spite of the sea.

Then came the moment we had dreaded. Ingrid was shown the room where she would live. I stood by the window staring at the ocean until we were ready to leave. Two nurses came to take care of Ingrid. Mama grasped Lilly's arm and drew her out into the corridor.

"You're going to stay here now, and Lilly will come with us," Papa said cheerfully.

Ingrid stood in the middle of her new room, her eyes on me, while behind her, waves crested and broke into foaming whitecaps far out at sea. She was very quiet. The nurses were prepared to give her a sedative if necessary. She looked at me the way she had when the snake was crawling up her hand and arm. Just before she gave it to me. Perhaps she understood what was happening.

"Take care, Ingrid," I said.

I touched her arm. Then we walked out of the room quickly, and the door closed behind us.

I left in a hurry. Down the stairs, through the corridors, across the gravel area by the entrance, and over to the car, where Lilly and Mama stood waiting. I started the engine, Papa got in beside me, Mama opened the back door and was about to get in too. We were so busy we didn't notice that Lilly had stopped a few meters from the car and was peering at us intently.

"Come, Lilly," Mama called. "We're leaving now."

"I don't want to go," said Lilly. "I want to stay here."

Mama went over, put her hand on Lilly's shoulder, and said something softly that only Lilly could hear. But then Lilly screamed. She tore herself loose from Mama and shrieked so loudly it resounded all through Nærlandsheimen.

"No!" she screamed. "No! No! No!"

We all realized it would be impossible.

We had to wait perhaps an hour to take care of the formalities. Papa and Mama sat in the director's office and signed several papers. Nurses had taken Lilly up to Ingrid's room. The two sisters were reunited, and a temporary room for Lilly was arranged. Mama explained about Lilly's fear of water and made sure her room had a view facing Nærbø and the hills beyond, so she wouldn't see the ocean. Perhaps she would be transferred to Bakkebø later; perhaps she would be able to stay at Nærlandsheimen with Ingrid and the others.

The director couldn't promise anything.

Meanwhile the sky had become overcast. I was sitting alone in the car when the rain started. Quietly and gently at first, just enough to cloud the windshield, then harder. The rain streamed down the glass in small, irregular rivulets. I sat there gazing out at the gray, pockmarked North Sea as the rain gradually increased, until finally it was whipping against the car.

At last we could leave. Mama and Papa stood under the small overhang outside the administration building and shook hands with the director while rain splattered the deserted front yard. They stood waiting for the downpour to end. But it didn't let up; I felt the wind seize the car, and rain drummed loudly on the hood. Finally, they had to run across the yard—Mama with her purse over her head, Papa with the contract papers in his hand. I started the engine, Papa got into the backseat, and Mama sat down next to me.

"Are we ready to go?" I asked.

"Yes," said Papa. "Everything is taken care of. Just go."

I turned in front of Stefanus church, which had long, dark water stains from the rain, and we came out onto the narrow road leading toward Nærbø. The windows fogged up, and I turned on the heater full blast. At first I drove slowly, in case Lilly changed her mind, in case she came running after us. I glanced in the rearview mirror, but saw nothing except sky and sea. Lilly did not change her mind. No one came running after us. We were alone on the road and I drove faster. Lilly stayed there, far out by the sea, together with Ingrid and her three brothers. After twenty-eight years Mama and Papa were free from caregiving at last. We didn't say anything. The rain blew in from the sea; I turned right at the first crossroad, and we headed home along the broad beaches of Jæren.

10.

I was finished at last. The house was empty, Mama's clothes had been sent to Russia, the Steinway piano had arrived safely at Astrid's apartment in Oslo, and I had found a new place for Herbert Andersson's painting. I'd taken the bag of Tone's clothes home with me. For a long time it just sat there, I didn't open it, nor did anyone else, and finally I put it away. *Tone's clothes* I wrote on the bag with an indelible pen. To whomever it might concern.

Two years went by.

It was December 1996. We had discovered that the house was in worse shape than we had thought. The roof leaked; when it rained the water ran down along the chimney, through Josef's room, and all the way down to the stove from Drammens Ironworks. Window putty cracked, a pane fell out one night with a west wind. Carpenter ants came in under the doorsill, and later into the kitchen. The deterioration had increased during the past two years. Rainwater must have run down between the walls for years, also when Mama lived there. Several beams had rotted. When the heat was turned off, large damp stains spread across the wallpaper in Josef's room, and also in Jensen and Matiassen's room. The doors warped and were difficult to close. I knew the house was drafty and poorly insulated; I remembered the rag rugs that froze to the floorboards, the burlap sacks that Papa cut into strips and stuffed around the windows, but I had no idea things were so bad. Astrid and I decided the house should be torn down. It had been Mama and Papa's dream to build their own asylum, their own little Dikemark, in the midst of the parish, far from the sea. Papa had perhaps imagined that the eleven happy years would continue, and Mama, who had never been there before, had dreamed of the house before we left Oslo in May 1940. In her mind she had seen the house standing at the edge of the woods. And when we finally arrived, she had to sit down on a stool in the middle of the empty room since she was six months pregnant; she had been quite overwhelmed, because the house was exactly as she had seen it in her dreams.

Perhaps that's how it was.

Astrid and I decided to have the house burned down, and the fire department gave us permission.

It was December 4. Mild, misty, a Wednesday. Astrid had returned to Oslo the night before. She couldn't bear to stay. I understood her, I'd have preferred to not be there too, but it would be worse to know the house was destroyed without my being there. I'd rather see it burn down.

The tops of the pine trees were blurred by the gray sky. There were four fire engines; two had backed onto the field far from the house, the other two were parked halfway down the hill, well shielded behind the hawthorn hedge. Fire hoses crisscrossed the yard in every direction. I stood a good distance away and drew my jacket tighter around me.

This would be a controlled burn.

All the doors and windows had been removed. Four men had carried out the wood-burning stove from Drammens Ironworks, and Josef's Jøtul stove tilted next to it in the grass. I saw the dancing couple and the black letters that once had branded Tone.

First they started several small blazes. They set fires and put them out maybe four, maybe five times. The last one in Josef's room. They let that burn until the flames burst out the window and the room was black and smoldering. Afterward there was a dark stripe up the paneling. Steam rose from the walls and water dripped from the ceiling beams, but the siblings' room was still unharmed. I was cold, my feet were freezing, but I wanted to stand there and watch.

After a few minutes' discussion, they decided to set the entire house on fire.

Two men went inside. They were away for a long time. I heard their voices in the front hall. I knew where they would light the fire: in the center of the house, in the little storeroom under the stairs where I'd found the tin plates and Matiassen's lantern. They were wearing smoke diver gear, and when they shouted to each other their voices became distorted through the masks. Finally, they appeared in the doorway, like two creatures from outer space. Everyone waited as the flames rose inside. I heard a crackling sound that slowly became louder. It grew stronger, wilder. Now and then we heard a crash, followed by a slight, sharp echo at the edge of the woods. Smoke came out of the roof and between gaps in the outside walls upstairs. The firemen stood ready with fire hoses, the generators hummed, and the water pumps shook the two closest fire trucks. More crashes were heard from inside the house. It sounded like something shattered and gave way; perhaps the entire stairway had collapsed. The flames were much bigger now. Great pillars of smoke emerged from Josef's window and from the two windows in Jensen and Matiassen's room. Smoke poured from the entire house, it gathered in a bluish-black column several meters above the roof and slowly drifted north on an imperceptible current of air. The flames first broke out of Josef's room, and about the same time the firemen sprayed powerful streams of water up the wall. For a moment the fire was beaten back, but soon the flames reappeared, and this time they had gathered force and broke through the roof. I was standing about forty meters away, but I felt the heat on my face, chest, and trousers. It was a scene I'd never imagined I would see. It was a scene I will never forget. Steam rose from the ground for several meters in all directions. One man was assigned to hose down the ash tree, but the heat from the house was so intense that thin wisps of smoke swirled from the outermost branches, like extinguished matches. It had taken months to build the house back then just before the war; it took minutes to burn it down. The walls were thin, the framework poor. I remembered how plainly I heard Jensen's conversations with Our Lord, and Mama's clear voice when she sang for Erling and Ingrid. I remembered how well you could hear someone climbing the stairs, how Tone and I lay in bed listening. Now I saw the framework appear behind the outer walls, and at one point I could see straight through the upstairs, from the charred remains of Josef's room to the treetops on the other side.

More minutes went by, the house was still standing. I moved a little closer. Steam rose from the sleeves of my jacket, I felt raindrops in my hair, and then suddenly the east side of the house collapsed. Half of the roof, as well as Jensen and Matiassen's room, plunged into the living room; a sea of sparks flew into the air, and afterward burning planks and beams lay everywhere. The west side of the house remained standing for a while longer. It was impossible to say what held it up. Everything was aflame. But it stayed upright for several more minutes before the siblings' room collapsed too, leaving the house below in ruins. The fire created an aureole in the mist. Only then did I notice Anna. She was standing in the garden outside her house. Lightly clad, only a thin cardigan over her shoulders. She stood watching, just like me. At first I considered going down there, but I didn't do that. We each stood alone and watched the house burn down.

Later I was told that the fire's aureole could be seen in most of the parish. First an aureole, then at last the house tore loose from the masonry and rose above the woods. The house rose higher and higher—even though, unlike the story I'd told Tone, nobody played the heavy Steinway piano, and Josef didn't strike a key.

Then it was gone.

The fire burned quietly for several more hours.

Dusk began to fall about three o'clock. At four-thirty the sky was completely dark, but flames still lit up one side of the ash tree. The ground was warm and dry, and I went over to look at the trunk more closely. The bark had opened on the side facing the house. They had hosed the tree continuously, but that hadn't been enough; the bark had pulled back, and I couldn't tell whether the tree was dead or alive.

Two firemen stayed through the evening. They sat in the fire engine's cab with the doors open, the radio on, and disco music streaming into the darkness. I stayed too. I felt I had to be there. The rain increased, acidic smoke hovered over the field, and soon there were no visible flames, just occasional flashes of glowing red timber under a layer of ash. The house was gone, only the two chimneys remained. They made it possible for me to picture the rooms and the stairway, the living room and the small bedroom and the kitchen, and how everything had been. We had all lived around these two black towers, but nobody had known that, and I was the only one who would see them still standing.

I returned the next day. Everything was burned out, the fire engines had left muddy tire tracks. I buttoned my jacket. The air was rancid from smoke and ashes. Then I heard footsteps coming up the road, and I knew who it was before I turned around.

"I never thought I'd see this," said Anna when she reached me.

"I didn't either," I replied.

"But maybe it was for the best," she added.

"Yes," I said. "I think so."

Then I showed her the ash tree, the long, gaping gash that began almost at the ground. It was as if the tree itself had opened, and this had happened despite the firemen hosing it down to save it. The gash in the tree was as wide as my hand.

"Do you think it will survive?" I said.

Anna placed her hand on the trunk.

"We won't know until spring," she said.

11.

A few weeks before Christmas the same year, I took the train westward from Kristiansand. I'd long thought I should visit them, but hadn't done so.

Not until now.

It was the same train route that Erling, Sverre, and Nils had taken so many times when they came home for Christmas and summer vacation. I saw the same landscape they must have seen; I glided slowly along the same gray Lake Lundevatnet, past the small railroad town of Moi, through wild mountain scenery with sheer precipices and dark canyons, until we neared the coast again at Egersund. I got off there and waited for the local train that would take me the final stretch to Nærbø station. In Egersund the snow had turned into rain and sleet; I stood on the platform with my back to the wind and both hands deep in my jacket pockets. After perhaps twenty minutes, the train arrived. I sat down in the last car and waited while the doors stood open and raindrops streamed down the windows, but no one else came aboard. I appeared to be riding alone along the Jæren coastline, and I had a clear view over the cold, bleak North Sea. It was an old train, with worn leather seats and swaying coat hangers by the doors, and it stopped at station after station without anyone getting on or off as far as I could tell.

At Nærbø station, I got off in wind and driving rain. I found a store nearby and bought five sweet buns, five bottles of soda, and a package of cookies.

From Nærbø I took a taxi out toward the sea and Nærlandsheimen. I remembered the fields, the stone fences that seemed to link the farms together in gray chains, and soon I saw the distinctive pyramid-shaped spire of Stefanus church.

I arranged for the driver to pick me up in two hours. Then I closed the door of the taxi, waited until it had driven away, and walked the final distance alone. Out here the wind was even stronger. The rain furiously pelted the bag of sodas and buns. I walked across the area in front of the Stone House and the former American Telegraph office. For almost fifty years Nærlandsheimen had been a home for the mentally disabled, but now the organization was phasing out. The siblings had moved to a row of small, identical houses that looked out toward the athletic field. My shoulders and trouser legs were wet, water seeped into my shoes.

They still lived together, with private rooms, it's true, but under the same roof, just as they had for most of their lives. The brothers no longer lived in a building for asocial, mentally disabled men. Ingrid no longer had a room with a splendid view of the sea. Lilly had not been transferred to Bakkebø, but she was still afraid of water. At first they were separated, but later were reunited in a building that resembled an ordinary house. There were five such houses in a row, essentially the same, except for different flower boxes on the terraces, different curtains in the windows, and different cars parked outside. The flower boxes, incidentally, were empty.

I knew which house was theirs; their names were on the mailbox outside, and I saw them through the large windows as I approached.

Lilly was now sixty-eight years old, Nils sixty-six, Sverre was fifty-five, and Ingrid was the same age as me.

One person was missing, however.

Erling had become increasingly sensitive during the past few years. His migraines had gotten worse, he couldn't stand to be with the other four. It was as if the sight of them made him more and more despondent. As if they constantly reminded him of himself. And that upset him. Finally, all he could tolerate was his own company. In the end, not even that. At the very end he just sat on a chair turned toward the wall, his head wobbling as if from a foolish, hopeless thought that haunted him constantly. Now Erling was at rest by the old Nærbø church. He lived to be sixty-one years old. He had not had a medal for courage nor a wandering cup in which to see himself.

Through the windows the four looked like any gathering of elderly or middle-aged people. They had already seen me. They waved through the windows as I walked up the driveway. I rang the bell, and Ingrid opened the door. She hugged me and held me tight, laughing loudly into my shoulder.

"It's wonderful to see you, Ingrid!" I said.

I took off my dripping jacket and wet shoes and went in to see the others. My socks left shiny footprints on the floor. Nils and Sverre came over and shook hands with me, one after the other. Lilly shook my hand too, and held it tight.

"Did you come in your car?" she asked.

"Not this time," I said. "This time I took the train."

"Was it nice?" she asked, without letting go of my hand.

I nodded.

"Were there lots of people?"

"No," I replied. "I was about the only one."

"The only one?"

"The only one," I said.

Then she let go of my hand.

The table was already set with glasses and small plates. I took the sweet buns out of the bag, lay one on each plate, and put a bottle of Solo soda next to it; after that we sat down at the table, all five of us. A few seconds of uncertainty followed; Sverre looked at Nils, Nils grinned and looked at Ingrid, Ingrid looked at Lilly, and Lilly looked at me.

"Perhaps we should sing the table grace?" I suggested.

So we sang, as we had so many times before, and Nils and Sverre sang with clear, childlike voices that seemed almost unchanged. It was as if time had stood still. I heard my own childish voice singing. I saw the old room upstairs: the five beds, the tin plates in front of us, the picture of Jesus holding a lamb. It was as if Mama had not yet come home from Oslo, Matiassen sat under the ash tree in the garden, and Josef lay on his back reading in his room next to us. We sang. Chills went down my spine. Afterward everyone was quiet.

"Please eat," said Lilly.

We sat for a long time eating in silence. I drank a soda and looked out the window. I asked them about little things, questions that could mostly be answered with *yes* or *no*. Now and then, *thank you.*

"I didn't find Asina in the store," I said. "But Solo is almost the same."

"Yes, Solo is almost the same," said Nils.

"I didn't find Gjende shortbread either," I said.

"That's okay," said Sverre.

"You like these cookies too?" I asked.

"We like everything!" said Nils.

Suddenly Lilly said:

"Ingrid can talk."

I looked up in surprise.

"Is that true?"

Ingrid looked at me with a shy smile.

"Is that true, Ingrid?" I repeated.

Once we had taken off our clothes in front of each other with no bashfulness or shame, we had waded out into the icy water, and she had made me feel completely free.

"Will you let me hear?" I said.

Ingrid opened her mouth, I saw her glistening tongue and how her lips and tongue formed a word. She repeated it many times, like a plea that came from a place deep within her. I just sat there watching her. She did her utmost.

"Asina," she said. "Asina. Asina. Asina."

I didn't know what more to say; I'd run out of questions, and the four of them didn't have anything more they wanted to know from me. I sat for quite a while thinking I should tell them that Mama was gone, and that the house at home no longer existed.

"It's a long time since all of you were home on vacation," I said.

"Yes," said Nils. "It's a long time."

"But you have a good life here too."

"We have a good life here too," said Sverre.

Another silence. It was as if they were waiting for me to come to the point. I opened the package of cookies and sent it around.

"Do you remember Tone?" I asked.

Nobody replied. Nils grinned as before. Ingrid licked around her mouth. Sverre looked at Lilly. Lilly looked at me.

"I had a sister named Tone," I went on. "She died the first summer after you came to us. But then I got a new sister, and she's named Astrid."

"She's not dead," said Lilly.

"No, she lives in Oslo," I said.

I felt I wanted to talk more about Tone, but didn't know what to say.

"Surely you remember Tone," I said to Lilly. "She was so fond of you."

Our eyes met. Once she had stood in the semidarkness and gazed lovingly at me, once she had sat on the edge of the bed and stroked my hair. Once I had almost been her child. Now she had grown old. Her hair was gray, but her eyes were clear.

"Of me?" she said.

"Yes," I replied. "Do you remember?"

And maybe it was a look on my face, in my eyes, something that made her see how deeply I wanted her to give a certain answer. The silence was unbearable for a moment. Then she said:

"Yes. I do. I remember now."

We sat together for another quarter of an hour. Another fierce rainstorm came in from the sea and beat against the tall windows; the wind howled in the kitchen exhaust fan. We drank our sodas, finished eating. Ingrid swept bits of coconut from the table into her hand and licked remnants of custard filling from inside the paper bag. Then Lilly got up from her chair. She cleared away the five plates and set them on the kitchen counter; next she picked up the bottles, even though everyone hadn't finished drinking, and put them in the sink. She found a dishcloth and wiped off the table while the rest of us sat watching her. No one protested. When she had finished, she turned to me.

"You need to leave, because we usually take a nap now."

I nodded.

"Of course."

I stood up slowly as everyone's eyes turned toward me; bits of coconut sprinkled from my lap, my trousers were not yet dry.

"It was nice to see all of you," I said.

Ingrid gazed at me attentively. Her eyes were so gentle. I wanted to hug her, but didn't.

"Well, I'll go now," I said.

I tied my shoes in the entry, zipped my jacket up to my chin, and called to them one last time before I left. Then I called to Ingrid.

"Ingrid," I called softly. Like a question.

It was the first time I'd called to her since that summer almost fifty years ago. I heard my childish voice shouting somewhere in the woods. I stood in the entry and waited, I looked toward the doorway with my heart pounding, but she didn't come.

Afterward I stood in the parking lot in front of the Stone House. The taxi wasn't due to pick me up for a while yet. Perhaps I should have told them that Mama had died, perhaps I should have told them that the house—their childhood home in a way—had burned to the ground. That everything was gone except the ash tree, that a gash had opened in its trunk and no one knew yet whether it would survive.

Perhaps I should have told them.

It was cold, the wind blew from the ocean, and it was still raining a little, but not so much that I got wetter than I already was. I put my hands in my pockets and started to walk along the road toward the sea. The ground was muddy, dirty brown water had collected in old tire tracks; the water shivered and shook in the wind.

It was perhaps two hundred meters to the ocean.

Near the end of the road I came to windblown sandbanks and brown tussocks with salt-scorched marram grass trembling in the breeze. To my right, the long, flat stretches of shoreline continued along the coast as far as I could see; to my left, I glimpsed the old Hå rectory and the red light at Obrestad lighthouse. I climbed down a sandbank until I stood on the beach itself. A belt of crackling seaweed lay several meters from the water's edge. I walked out to where the sand was wet and compact and the waves sent avalanches of frothy foam almost to my shoes. For a long time I stood there, taking deep, calm breaths. The iron-blue North Sea curved along the horizon and continued endlessly. It was overwhelming. The rain stopped, my hair was wet, the wind tasted salty. Nothing held me back. Then the tears began to fall.

PART SIX

One afternoon before Christmas, Ingrid and I were in Josef's room watching him polish the medal for courage. He had borrowed silver polish and a chamois, and the medal got so shiny you could see yourself in it.

"Look," said Josef, showing us. "When it's like a mirror, it's exactly the way it should be."

He held the medal in front of me. It turned slowly, and I actually saw myself, my own face, slightly distorted in the silver.

"And now you," he said to Ingrid.

He held the medal in front of her so she could see herself, but Ingrid refused. She turned away, looked at me, and waited to see what I would say. But I didn't say anything. I went over to the window, and then I caught sight of some people walking up the road. It was as though the early darkness had gathered all its strength in order to conjure up two gray figures out of all the snowy whiteness. When they got closer I saw it was Mama and Anna. They had shawls over their heads and walked arm in arm, their shoulders were covered with snow, and I knew they had been to the church to practice for the concert. Their wavering tracks stretched behind them, and then disappeared in the twilight. I heard them stamp their feet on the front steps, Anna brushed the snow off her shoes with a broom, and when they finally closed the outer door Josef, Ingrid, and I already stood in the front hall.

"I thought two angels had arrived," said Josef.

"Oh, just wait till we've shaken off the feathers," said Mama.

Josef's eyes grew wide, and Mama laughed as melting snow dripped from her shawl.

The last day before Christmas break I sat at my desk in the Hønemyr schoolhouse. I heard the sound of pen nibs scratching on paper, and at one point I raised my eyes and looked out the window. It had started to snow again. Large, wet flakes drifted down slowly from the unchanging sky. The snowfall steadily increased, the forest shimmered through the snowflakes, and I put down my pen and just watched.

Suddenly, Nils Apesland stood by my desk.

"Say hello to Ingrid, and wish her Merry Christmas," he said.

I looked at him and nodded.

"I'll do that."

It was still snowing when I went to bed that evening. The night-light glowed on my bedside table and I didn't want to turn it off. I lay staring at it until my eyes hurt, and fell asleep with it still on. In the middle of the night the light awakened me. I heard footsteps outside my door, the handle went down, and Mama entered.

"Are you asleep?" she whispered.

"No," I replied.

She walked quietly across the room to the window and opened the curtains.

"Is it still snowing?" I asked.

"Yes," she said. "Harder than ever."

She stood at the foot of my bed looking at me. She seemed large and heavy, her shadow went far up the wall.

"Am I going to get a sister?" I asked.

I didn't dare to look at her.

"Yes," she said. "Or a brother."

There was a long pause.

"Are you going to sing in church?"

She nodded. I said no more, and she just stood there.

"Should I turn out the light?" she said finally.

I nodded. She came over, switched off the lamp, and the room became almost completely dark.

"Go to sleep now," she said.

I closed my eyes. She sat down on the edge of the bed. I sensed her smell. I sensed her heaviness.

"I will," I said.

She kept sitting there. She touched my arm. Finally I opened my eyes, but at that moment she rose and walked toward the half-open door. I heard her footsteps in the hall. In my mind I saw the snow falling outside the window, I saw it falling through the roof upstairs, through the floor in Jensen and Matiassen's room, and down into my dreams.

"I'll go to sleep now," I said.

The next morning the pine trees bowed under heavy snow, they leaned toward each other as if talking of bygone days; our horse plodded down the road while Papa walked beside the sleigh in waist-deep snow.

In the evening the stars came out. Josef stood by the window peering at the ash tree, at the black branches that were so thin the snow hadn't stuck to them. He saw the moon, Venus, and maybe Orion above the bowing pine trees in the south.

"Look," he said. "The pine trees are saying their evening prayers."

Early on the afternoon of December 23, Mama left home before the rest of us. Joseph watched her as she stood tying her shawl by the mirror in the front hall.

"Do I look respectable, Josef?" she asked.

Josef thought for a moment.

"The missus is extremely respectable," he said. "Extremely respectable."

Papa hitched up the horse. He stamped the snow off his feet on the front steps, stuck his head in the door and shouted that the sleigh was ready, and they drove off to the church while it was still light.

Papa returned before dusk and went upstairs to take care of Jensen and Matiassen; I heard their voices through the floor. Afterward I went to the siblings' room with him. Before she left, Mama had helped Lilly clean the room; there were new curtains in the windows, a Christmas cloth with embroidered sleigh bells on the table, and Papa had chopped down a pine tree that they had decorated. The five of them sat around the table, but they had finished eating. The plates had been carried down to the kitchen. The table wiped off. Everyone looked up. Erling burped.

"We're leaving now," said Papa.

"Going where?" Lilly asked.

"We'll be back before bedtime," Papa said briefly. He closed the door, turned to me, and was about to go downstairs.

"No," I said.

Papa looked at me in surprise.

"Why can't they come along?" I said.

Papa just looked at me.

"I want them to come along."

Standing outside the siblings' room, we heard them singing the table grace, even though they had just eaten. They sang on the other side of the door, and there must have been a look on my face that made Papa hesitate.

"The horse can't pull so many in the sleigh," he said.

"We can take two trips."

"There's not enough time."

"Yes, there is," I said. "If we hurry."

Josef and I stood on the front steps waiting while Papa led the horse across the yard. We saw light in the two low windows of the cattle barn, and just beneath them, the glow of two other windows floating in the snow. It was so dark I could only sense the horse as a large, living shadow that glided toward us next to Papa. Josef held

Matiassen's lantern at shoulder height while Papa hitched up the sleigh. As we left I saw light in Jensen and Matiassen's window; in the window facing south I saw Lilly, Ingrid, and Nils; Erling and Sverre were in the window facing west.

Lilly had been told to get everyone ready.

I huddled close to Josef while Papa sat on empty sacks in front of us with the reins gathered in his hand and the flaps on his fur cap firmly down over his ears. The night smelled of horse and coldness, the harness creaked, the sleigh runners whizzed beneath us. We passed Sløgedal's house, which was completely dark; at the river Papa turned the horse west, and we glided across the open countryside toward Breivoll. Continuing north, we soon saw lights from other sleighs behind us. When we arrived at the church, Papa turned the horse around and went back to pick up the siblings. The vestibule door was open, creating a yellow strip of light on the snow-covered churchyard. Josef and I followed the narrow path that had been shoveled from the churchyard entrance to the steps of the church; there we stopped and waited. Everything was white and still. No gravestones were visible. I noticed Josef looking at me. Even in the dark I knew where her grave was.

Josef and I stood on the steps as people came up the path and disappeared into the church.

"Welcome, welcome," Josef said to people as they arrived. "You know me, don't you? Former tenor in the Hope Chorus. Glad to see you. Glad to see you."

After a while we got cold standing there, after a while no one else came up the path; finally, only Papa and the siblings were missing.

We saw the glow of Matiassen's lantern, a blue, unearthly light gliding past the snowbanks as they approached. Papa drove the horse all the way to the churchyard wall. The five siblings were huddled together, buried in woolen blankets with only their heads sticking out, as if someone were trying to smuggle them through the darkness. Papa fastened the oat bag on the horse, Nils helped him with the horse blanket, then all five scurried through the snow after Papa.

They barely made it.

"So the crazies are here too," said Josef.

Ingrid's cheeks were rosy from the sleigh ride, her nose was running and she wiped it with the arm of her coat. As the flock of siblings came stamping into the vestibule, Sløgedal stood by the door and greeted them in surprise.

"You're coming in full force this evening," he said.

"Yes indeed," said Papa. "If there's a concert, then there's a concert."

Sløgedal nodded and put his hand on Papa's shoulder; then he handed out the evening's program, and we went into the warm sanctuary.

The church smelled of smoke and the pleasant warmth of a summer long past. The raging fire in the woodstove crackled and sputtered up the metal pipe. People were sitting in the pews, and Josef nodded right and left as we walked up the middle aisle. First Josef, then Papa and I, and behind us came all five siblings. Josef went up to his place by the pulpit, opened the little door at the end of the pew, and let the rest of us in. I sat between Papa and Lilly. She had her hands in her lap, and I glanced down at the hand that had stroked my hair. We sat in exactly the same place as during the baptism five years earlier, and in exactly the same place as during the funeral just a few months ago.

We had no more than sat down before Anna began to play the reed organ up in the organ loft. First softly, sort of hesitantly, but then the notes grew louder and began to sparkle as they drifted down over everyone there.

When the organ music ended, Alma Kleveland came forward to read the Christmas prologue. I looked at the candles, which were bright and holy and cast a reddish glow through the pages she was reading from. When she finished, everyone sang "Beautiful Savior."

After that the leader of the Mission Society, Syvert Mæsel, gave a short talk, and then Nils Apesland read the entire Christmas gospel by candlelight. The church was silent except for his monotonous voice, the fire burning furiously in the woodstove, and the flies, revived by the surprising warmth, buzzing blindly toward the window just above God's eye.

When Nils Apesland finished, he closed the Bible and came down to sit with the rest of us. I realized that now was the moment it would happen. Anna played a short prelude. I felt the blood pounding in my ears. Josef cleared his throat, Papa straightened up. Erling's head wobbled and he laughed a little to himself, until both Lilly and Nils hushed him.

Then she came.

She walked calmly out of a door hidden behind the altar painting. Holding the music in her hand, she stopped next to the baptismal font and raised her eyes, but she didn't seem to see that we were sitting right in front of her. She didn't see that we had brought all the siblings. Instead she looked up at Anna, perhaps their eyes met in the organ mirror. Everyone knew Mama had screamed that time Lilly stood out in the river, everyone knew Tone lay under the snow with a red bow in her hair and white carnations in her hands. And at that moment, while the candles flickered and Mama took a deep breath, everyone in the church saw that she was going to have another child.

Mama stood there under the Roman arches and sang as I'd never heard her sing before. I closed my eyes, and saw her standing on the sandbar waving to us. I saw her walking up the road from the milk platform with Papa. I saw Papa carrying her suitcase as she clutched his arm, and then I saw her enter my bedroom; she turned out the night-light and just sat there until I opened my eyes, and at that moment she got up and left.

Mama stood singing only a few meters in front of us, but it wasn't she who stood there. It was the person she perhaps really should have been. The person she was on the way to becoming when she suddenly stopped taking voice lessons in Oslo. The person she was on the way to becoming before she changed course abruptly, became a nurse at Ullevål hospital, applied at Dikemark, met Papa, and went with him to the end of the world. Now she stood there singing. Anna played, and perhaps she glanced in the organ mirror and looked at Mama too. Everyone sat as if paralyzed, gazing at her. The whole congregation, all the siblings, Papa, Josef, and I. And at that moment I heard Tone whisper: *Listen, Mama is singing!*

The fire no longer burned in the woodstove, only embers and white ashes remained. The concert was over, people got up from the pews, and I felt a cold draft coming all the way from the vestibule. The candles were still burning, but the flames flickered, the wax dripped, and soon Sløgedal came and blew out the candles one by one. Then he shook Papa's hand.

"We'll never forget this," he said.

"Neither will I," Papa replied.

Sløgedal stood there holding Papa's hand and didn't know what else to say, but I knew that after this nothing would be the same again.

Anna climbed down the steep stairs from the organ loft; the sheriff came over, he too put a hand on Papa's shoulder, and as always, Josef made sure he stood next to the sheriff. Everyone wanted to greet Papa, and everyone was waiting for Mama to come out from the sacristy. But she didn't come. When she had finished singing, she disappeared through the door behind the altar painting. After a while people began to move down the middle aisle; I felt the winter cold seeping from the walls now that the stove was no longer burning. Papa turned to Anna.

"I think you'd better go and see how she is," he said.

Anna disappeared behind the altar painting and was gone for a long time. I don't know what happened. I don't know what took such a long time. But finally both Mama and Anna appeared by the altar railing. Papa took a step forward, perhaps he shook his head slightly, perhaps he smiled. I don't know. In any case, Mama smiled; I saw that, and I thought the reason Papa stood there under the Roman arches was because he was the only person in this world who could receive that smile.

"Come," said Papa. "Let's go home now."

They stood for a moment by the altar railing, while Ingrid and I and the other siblings walked down the middle aisle, across the doorsill, and out into the bitterly cold vestibule. The church door was wide open, frost glittered on the inside, and I caught a glimpse of the shoveled path that disappeared into the darkness. We paused, and I turned to look back into the church. Mama and Papa stood together by the chancel, Josef helped Anna with her coat, Hans withdrew to the side and ran his hand slowly through his hair. Then they came down the aisle, all five of them. Mama moved heavily, she held Papa's arm and her eyes had a warm, elated glow. I saw it as I stood there on the threshold of the sanctuary with the cold air at my back. We all saw it. Ingrid howled softly, but quieted when I took her hand. Lilly held Sverre in her arms, Josef went to stand beside her, Erling did the same, and Nils put his hands deep into his pockets. We stood peering into the lighted sanctuary. We just stood there, all of us, waiting for Mama to come.

GAUTE HEIVOLL is the author of *Before I Burn* (Graywolf Press, 2014), which won the Brage Prize and was a finalist for the Critics Prize and the Booksellers' Prize in Norway. He studied creative writing at Telemark College, law at the University of Oslo, and psychology at the University of Bergen. He lives in Norway.

NADIA CHRISTENSEN has published literary translations of seventeen books, including two winners of the Pegasus Prize for Literature. A former director of publications at the American-Scandinavian Foundation in New York City, she established the foundation's annual prize for literary translation into English from Nordic languages. In 1996 King Harald of Norway knighted her for her contribution to US-Norway relations.

The text of *Across the China Sea* is set in Minion Pro. Book design by Rachel Holscher. Composition by Bookmobile Design and Digital Publisher Services, Minneapolis, Minnesota. Manufactured by Versa Press on acid-free, 30 percent postconsumer wastepaper.